FLYAWAY VACATION SWEEPSTAKES!

This month's destination:

Exciting ORLANDO, FLORIDA!

Are you the lucky person who will win a free trip to Orlando? Imagine how much fun it would be to visit Walt Disney World**, Universal Studios**, Cape Canaveral and the other sights and attractions in this area! The Next page contains tow Official Entry Coupons, as does each of the other books you received this shipment. Complete and return *all* the entry coupons—the more times you enter, the better your chances of winning!

Then keep your fingers crossed, because you'll find out by October 15, 1995 if you're the winner! If you are, here's what you'll get:

- Round-trip airfare for two to Orlando!
- 4 days/3 nights at a first-class resort hotel!
- $500.00 pocket money for meals and sightseeing!

Remember: The more times you enter, the better your chances of winning!*

*NO PURCHASE OR OBLIGATION TO CONTINUE BEING A SUBSCRIBER NECESSARY TO ENTER. SEE BACK PAGE FOR ALTERNATIVE MEANS OF ENTRY AND RULES.

**THE PROPRIETORS OF THE TRADEMARKS ARE NOT ASSOCIATED WITH THIS PROMOTION.

VOR KAL

FLYAWAY VACATION
SWEEPSTAKES
OFFICIAL ENTRY COUPON

This entry must be received by: SEPTEMBER 30, 1995
This month's winner will be notified by: OCTOBER 15, 1995
Trip must be taken between: NOVEMBER 30, 1995-NOVEMBER 30, 1996

YES, I want to win the vacation for two to Orlando, Florida. I understand the prize includes round-trip airfare, first-class hotel and $500.00 spending money. Please let me know if I'm the winner!

Name_____

Address _____ Apt. _____

City   State/Prov.   Zip/Postal Code

Account #_____

Return entry with invoice in reply envelope.

© 1995 HARLEQUIN ENTERPRISES LTD.   COR KAL

FLYAWAY VACATION
SWEEPSTAKES
OFFICIAL ENTRY COUPON

This entry must be received by: SEPTEMBER 30, 1995
This month's winner will be notified by: OCTOBER 15, 1995
Trip must be taken between: NOVEMBER 30, 1995-NOVEMBER 30, 1996

YES, I want to win the vacation for two to Orlando, Florida. I understand the prize includes round-trip airfare, first-class hotel and $500.00 spending money. Please let me know if I'm the winner!

Name_____

Address _____ Apt. _____

City   State/Prov.   Zip/Postal Code

Account #_____

Return entry with invoice in reply envelope.

© 1995 HARLEQUIN ENTERPRISES LTD.   COR KAL

They'd spend the night together

Logan didn't need to say the words; Tara knew. And the thought kindled a glow inside her that had nothing to do with the crackling fireplace.

One hand she held out to the fire for warmth, the other stroked her sleeping son's downy head as it rested on her leg. Logan's gaze moved from the child to her slightly trembling hands, to the swell of her breasts under her sweater.

Pulse racing, she wiped her palm on her thigh and searched for conversation. "Are you hungry?"

"Not for food."

She didn't dare ask what he was hungry for. The answer was plain as the passion on his face. But she couldn't stop herself from asking, "What are you thinking?"

"How long it's been since I've wanted a woman," he replied. "And now I want you."

Dear Reader,

Be prepared to meet another "Woman of Mystery"!

This month we're proud to bring you another book in our ongoing WOMAN OF MYSTERY program, designed to bring you the books of authors new to Intrigue.

Meet Susan Kearney, author of *Tara's Child*.

Susan likes suspense-packed romance with an unforgettable twist. She's also more than fond of feisty heroines and heroes with soft hearts and hard heads. Sue lives in Florida with her husband, two children and two Boston terriers.

We're dedicated to bringing you the best new authors, the freshest new voices. Be on the lookout for more "women of mystery."

Regards,

Debra Matteucci
Senior Editor and Editorial Coodinator
Harlequin Books
300 East 42nd Street
New York, NY 10017

Tara's Child
Susan Kearney

Harlequin Books

TORONTO • NEW YORK • LONDON
AMSTERDAM • PARIS • SYDNEY • HAMBURG
STOCKHOLM • ATHENS • TOKYO • MILAN
MADRID • WARSAW • BUDAPEST • AUCKLAND

For my children, with love,
from a mom that burns chicken noodle soup

ISBN 0-373-22340-4

TARA'S CHILD

Copyright © 1995 by Susan Hope Kearney

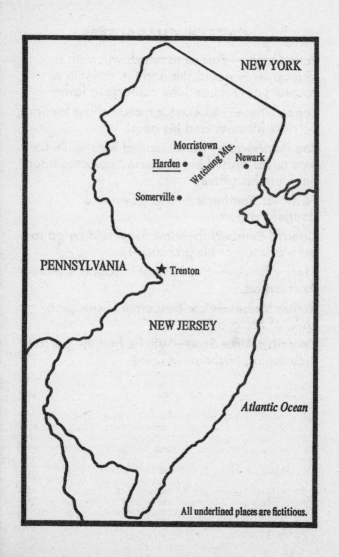

NEW YORK

Morristown

Harden • • Newark
Watchung Mts.

Somerville •

PENNSYLVANIA
★ Trenton

NEW JERSEY

Atlantic Ocean

All underlined places are fictitious.

CAST OF CHARACTERS

Tara Larson—Forced to match wits with a kidnapper—would she find the strength to protect her child and the courage to love?

Logan Stone—An ex-stuntman. Falling for Tara, he risks his neck and his heart.

Joe Pemberton—He tormented Tara while he was alive. Would her deceased husband haunt her from his grave?

Nicholas Pemberton—The pawn in a dangerous game.

Conrad Pemberton—How far would he go to gain custody of his grandson?

Marge Henley—Her interest in Logan is more than casual.

Ruthie Raines—How desperate is she for a child of her own?

Detective Mike Scott—Will he find the person threatening Nicholas in time?

Prologue

Damn the blizzard! The lace curtain dropped across the windowpane, obscuring the winter storm that raged outside. An added complication, and just when the plan was coming to fruition. Soon the baby would be where he belonged, instead of with *that* woman, who had never even gone to college and couldn't hold a job.

The dusty gilt mirror in the silent hall reflected a satisfied grin. The rooms of the old Victorian house hadn't always been so quiet. A few years ago they'd echoed with the sounds of happy laughter ringing off the polished oak floors. At the grand piano, concert pianists had accompanied violinists during lavish parties. The scent of spring roses had wafted through the air with the promise of summer passion.

Gone. Lost with a turn of the seasons.

The winter wind howled and meshed with the pain of a wounded heart. At the memories of things lost, a fist sent a crystal vase of long-dead flowers crashing to the floor. One withered bud clung stubbornly to a picture frame. Heedless of the fragile stem, shaking fingers plucked the daisy and dropped the desiccated petals to the floor, to be crushed to dust beneath a vicious heel.

Two years was a long time to wait for revenge. Rage flooded icy fingers with the heat of purpose. Revenge. And a chance to set things right.

A clenched hand lifted a crisp handkerchief to lips tight with determination. All of the special arrangements had worked out so well, better than expected, with each part planned to the tiniest detail. Except for the sudden change in weather.

However, delays could not be tolerated. Now was the time to strike terror in the heart of the enemy. Sneaking into the house and snatching the baby shouldn't be a problem, not with the locksmith tools in the car. And soon the money would fall into place, too.

With renewed strength, a gloved hand opened the door into the bitter wind. Snow might make the task more difficult, but it would also hide the tracks. A face tipped up to the sleet and welcomed the bite of stinging cold.

The blizzard was going to expedite the plan, after all.

Chapter One

A knock thundered on the front door. Startled, Tara Larson spilled her hot chocolate across the kitchen table. Where had she packed the paper towels? Searching for a towel to mop up the mess before it bled into the newspaper, she plunged her hand into a half-opened box.

Another loud bang sounded on the door. She quickly blotted up the liquid with toilet tissue, the only paper she could find.

"I'm coming!" She ran to the door, drying her hands on her jeans.

Wind whipped the bare branches of the oak trees against the front of the house, and a keening whistle blew outside. Tara froze, then laughed at herself. No need to worry. The noises of this place were just new to her, and the eerie sound was just the house groaning under the wind's whip.

Unlocking the dead bolt, but keeping the chain latched, she opened the door a crack. Outside, winter skies formed a gray dome over the New Jersey neighborhood, where houses in the subdivision stood dreary and drab, like a newspaper picture with its many tints of gray. A dark silhouette loomed across her doorway. "Who is it?"

"Logan Stone."

"Who?"

"Barbara said you'd expect me."

Tara sighed. Leave it to Barbara's relative to drive out with a major snowstorm predicted. She hoped he wouldn't mind that she'd changed her mind about redecorating, because she had a more practical use for this man's time.

"Can I see some identification, please?"

He set down his tool chest, reached into his back pocket and handed her a business card. Sure enough, it read Logan Stone, Residential Construction and Renovation. We Aim to Please.

She fumbled with the chain. An icy gust caught the door, and it blew open with a blast of frigid air. Rubbing her arms against the chill, Tara took a step backward, but kept her gaze on Logan, curious to see what he looked like behind his hat and muffler. He bent over, wiping his snowy work boots on the welcome mat, so she could see only the top of his red wool hat.

"Come in."

During their last phone call, her best friend, Barbara, had chuckled mysteriously when she'd insisted on hiring Logan Stone to paint and paper Nicholas's room. "Think of him, I mean his work, as a housewarming present," Barbara had suggested. Her too-innocent coyness convinced Tara that her old friend was bent upon matchmaking.

Tara sighed. The next-to-last thing she wanted was more charity from Barbara. Her friend wouldn't even accept rent, claiming Tara was doing her a favor protecting the house from vandals while she worked the Paris–London air route for the next year. Right now, the *last* thing Tara wanted was a man inside the house, touching her belongings, asking her questions.

"If you live in my home," Barbara had said, "you have to make it cheerful for my godchild. Besides, Logan is my favorite cousin. Trust him."

And now the man Barbara had spoken about with such enthusiasm picked up his tool chest, took the two brick steps in one stride and invaded her foyer. Tara's gaze automatically focused on the spot where she expected his face to be. Instead, she confronted a broad chest and broader shoulders straining the fabric of his leather parka. Readjusting, she craned her neck back.

Though Logan Stone stood over six-and-a-half feet tall, she noticed his intense, black eyes right off. A forceful sensuality radiated from his cool stare, which made him seem as if he were looking not *at* her, but *into* her. But something more than his size and demeanor threatened her newly won self-confidence. His hard features were too dark, too arrogant, for her to feel comfortable.

He closed the door, relocking and chaining it, trapping her inside with him. His masculine scent, mingled with the leather of his jacket, surrounded her, and the foyer suddenly seemed cramped. It was all she could do not to step back when he offered his hand.

Courage. *The first day of the rest of my life.*

She hadn't touched a man in ten months. But she lifted her chin, and—while she didn't dare meet his gaze—she focused on his high cheekbones, nipped with the winter cold, and offered her hand.

When their palms pressed in the simple handshake, a spark sizzled up her arm. The contact was so brief she wondered if she was imagining things.

"Tara Larson?" At her nod, he continued, "I called last week—"

"I just moved in two days ago."

An expression of curiosity passed fleetingly over his face. What exactly had her friend told him about her?

He removed his jacket and slung it over one shoulder, using his index finger as a hook. A red-and-black flannel shirt emphasized his flat stomach and the power of his chest and muscular arms. When he removed his cap, thick black hair curled around the collar of his shirt. Faded black jeans with the seams slightly frayed, tucked into thick-soled work boots, encased powerful legs, slim hips.

What had Barbara said? Strong, dark, silent... and wild. Perhaps his reticence meant he wouldn't bother her with too many questions. He wouldn't be here long enough for her to have to worry about the wild part—she hoped.

His harsh baritone woke her from her thoughts like a cold shower. "Let's go to the bedroom."

"Excuse me?" So much for polite conversation. While Barbara had an odd collection of family and friends, they usually had a modicum of manners.

He raked a hand through his thick, dark hair. "The wallpaper for the child's room? I promised Barbara I'd hang it this week."

"Oh." Blood heated her cheeks. Why did every man alive succeed in making her feel foolish? First Joe, now... She took a deep breath.

The first day of the rest of my life.

She would never have to put up with an overbearing man again, she reminded herself. "I didn't buy the wallpaper."

He frowned. "I suppose I could start with the paint."

"I didn't buy paint, either."

His broad shoulders stiffened. "Look, lady—"

"Tara."

He started to shrug into his jacket as if to leave. "You have my card. Call me when you're ready and I'll see if I can fit you into my schedule."

"I want you to childproof the house, instead."

He set down the toolbox with a thump. When he said nothing but continued to stare with a raised eyebrow, she took his jacket and hung it over the doorknob. "I bought all the hardware. I have a list in the kitchen of what I need done."

"Lady, I don't childproof houses. I build them."

"Then you should be more than qualified for what I have in mind."

He shot her a penetrating look and folded his arms across his chest. "I'm qualified. That's not the point."

Frustration rose in her voice. "The job should be easy for someone with your experience. Don't you have the right equipment?"

"I assure you, I've all the proper equipment," he drawled with distinct mockery and a twinkle in his eyes.

Heat stole into her face, but she wouldn't back down an inch. "Then, what's the problem?"

"I only agreed to take this job as a favor to Barbara. My cousin paid me top dollar to paint and paper. Anybody with a screwdriver, perhaps your husband—''

"I'm a widow."

Logan returned her look unwaveringly, not even having the grace to look abashed, though he did give her an off-hand apology. "Sorry. Barbara didn't mention that."

"She told me that she paid for a week's worth of labor, and making this house safe is more important than changing the decor. If you don't want to work, why don't you give me back Barbara's money and I'll hire someone else?"

His response was impossibly calm. "Are you trying to manipulate me?"

She smiled at the thought. "Am I succeeding? I don't know anyone else in town, but—"

Picking up his tool box in one smooth motion, he limped straight into the kitchen, indicating he knew the house well. She followed, at first thinking his heavy tool chest pulled his body to one side, but then she realized his swagger had nothing to do with the weight of the tool chest. The imperfection made him appear more human and less like a model.

Logan led the way into the light and airy, newly re-modeled kitchen that opened into the den. She watched him scan the room, saw his lip curl at the wads of toilet tissue soaking up spilled chocolate be-fore his gaze moved on to the cartons cluttering the white tile floor.

Tara twisted one hand inside the other, realized her actions revealed her nervousness, and reminded her-self she had no need to apologize. Dropping her hands to her sides, she stiffened in defiance. "You'll have to work around the mess."

He shrugged. "It's not in my way."

Had it been Joe in her kitchen, she would have seen anger in his eyes. For a time, her dead husband and his impossible expectations had haunted her dreams and stalked her waking hours. She'd thought every man, no matter how tall or short, thin or heavy, looked and behaved like Joe. He'd been the man on every street corner, the man behind the wheel of each passing car. Leaving her apartment became an ordeal.

Moving to this new town, thirty miles from her last residence, would help her gain distance from her unhappy memories. Luckily, she'd come to realize not all men were like Joe. But still, having Logan, so big, so sure of himself, dominating her kitchen with his size, made her nervous.

Tara couldn't believe she'd stood up to him in the hallway. But ten months of soul-searching had strengthened her. Never again would she use a man's approval as the compass that steered her life. Not even a man as handsome as Logan Stone.

He was huge, drop-dead gorgeous, and to make her feel even more uncomfortable, his eyes had a startling intensity. And right now, those bold eyes centered on her, making her extremely aware of his masculine vitality.

Realizing he was waiting for her list, Tara gave herself a mental shake. Patting the top of a box as she passed by, she anticipated unpacking. A new start. She could put her things in any room she pleased, have Logan Stone fix the house any way she wanted.

She opened a kitchen drawer, handed him the baby-proofing list she'd cut from the newspaper, then gestured to the counter. "The hardware is in that bag."

From the back room, Nicholas called out. "Mama!"

"Excuse me." Turning on her heel, she raced down the hall, a nameless apprehension gripping her the instant she'd heard her son's voice. She'd have preferred to keep the baby in her room, but she'd read somewhere it wasn't healthy. And she couldn't afford to make any more mistakes—not with her precious child.

It took three times as many steps than she was accustomed to to reach Nicholas's room. In her old one-room apartment, where she'd lived the last nine months, he'd never slept more than a few feet away. But this house had narrow hallways and thick walls. Except for the kitchen that opened onto the den, the huge house seemed more claustrophobic than her tiny loft.

Finally, she reached the bedroom. With a damp grip she turned the knob quietly, pushed open the door and peered into Nicholas's crib.

Her son stood bouncing on his mattress as if on a trampoline. "Hi."

The sight of his sturdy arms and chubby legs pushed her fear back, and the possibility of danger floated away with every breath Nicholas took. Giving in to the need to feel his cuddly little body, she reached into the crib for him and inhaled the scent of baby lotion and powder, letting the softness of his tender skin reassure her.

He needed a change. "Mama's right here, darling."

"Is everything all right?" Logan's husky voice made her jerk.

She turned to face him, braced for expected ridicule over her unwarranted alarm. His mouth tightened into a thin, grim line, and he held the bag of hardware loosely in one hand, a hammer clenched in the other.

As she gazed at the tool and tried to still her racing heart, he lowered his arm. "When you took off like that I thought something might be wrong."

"I'm a little edgy, I guess." Seemingly picking up on her anxiety, Nicholas clutched her tightly. She handed him his favorite toy dinosaur.

Logan speared her with a disapproving stare that reminded her of how Joe had constantly criticized the way she cared for their son. She'd moved to Harden to forget her dead husband and make a new start in life. But at a time like this, it seemed there was no escape.

She patted Nicholas on the back, calming him. "I just finished reading a newspaper article about a baby being stolen from the bedroom while the mother cooked dinner. When he screamed—"

"You panicked."

"I was concerned."

"Yeah. Right." He stepped closer. "What's the little guy's name?"

"Nicholas."

"Hello, Nicholas. How old are you?" Logan greeted the child with a wide smile, and she lost her breath at the sudden transformation of Logan's face. When he grinned like that, the rigid edge disap-

peared, the harsh line of his cheekbones softened, and
his eyes looked almost friendly.

"He can only say a few words. He's almost a year
old."

Tara put Nicholas on the changing table and un-
snapped his pajamas. As usual, her son squirmed,
dropping his green dinosaur, reaching for other toys,
and making her task twice as difficult. Logan handed
him a blue plastic car, and Nicholas promptly put it in
his mouth.

"Thanks. The only time this kid holds still is when
he's asleep."

As she changed him, Logan watched over her
shoulder. "Is he walking?"

"I imagine he will very soon. Right now, he still
holds on to the furniture."

"He hasn't climbed out of the crib?"

"Don't give him any ideas." She frowned. Had Joe
been asking these questions about Nicholas's habits in
such minute detail, she'd have been worried she'd
forgotten some item on her husband's long list of
child-care instructions. Even though she knew Logan's questions came from the task she had asked him
to do, his queries brought back bad memories.

Although he'd done nothing but try to help, Logan's presence in the bedroom suddenly disturbed her.
The dark, shadowy spaces in the room shrank. Her
pulse rate shot up with him looming near her shoulder, and until he stepped over to the window, she felt
crowded.

While she dressed Nicholas in a shirt and coveralls,
Logan crouched by an electrical socket. As the dis-

tance between them increased, she allowed herself to relax.

Recalling the tingle of his touch when they shook hands, she knew better than to think she was attracted to Logan simply because she longed for male company. With his husky scent stirring feelings of vulnerable awareness she'd never had before, he appealed to her on a primitive level that unnerved her. He moved gracefully, his limp emphasizing the narrowness of his hips. And his big hands, with his long, supple fingers, held a strange appeal. She found herself staring whenever his back was to her. Right now he was taking a piece of white plastic out of the bag of hardware, wedging the device into the electrical outlet.

"Barbara said you can fix anything."

"Just about."

"So I'm glad the job will be done right."

"I aim to please."

She wouldn't touch that remark with a ten-foot pole. His gaze flicked over her boldly, flirtatiously, and she suspected his good looks had charmed countless women. Well, it wouldn't work with her. She might find him attractive—okay, gorgeous—but she and Nicholas were doing just fine by themselves, and she wouldn't allow any man to upset their lives.

"Are all these precautions necessary?" he grumbled.

"No one can watch a child every second." She stared at him, daring him to dispute her words, then wondered why she bothered justifying her actions to him. He merely grunted. Obviously Logan Stone knew nothing about kids. "You don't have children, do you?"

"Nope," he stated flatly. An inexplicable blankness came over his face. Apparently finished with the conversation, Logan left the bedroom for the hall.

Tara hugged the precious bundle that was her son, unable to imagine life without him. During the last eight months, she'd been fired from her job because of Nicholas, moved twice for Nicholas, and spent almost the last of her funds to keep her son safe. Logan wouldn't know how much a child meant until he had one of his own.

She swung her squirming son onto her hip.

"Down," he insisted.

With one last kiss, she placed him on the floor and let him crawl. He chased after Logan, who was moving along the hallway plugging electrical sockets while she followed slowly, keeping a watchful gaze on her son.

Logan paused halfway down the narrow hall. "Is this the bathroom?"

When she nodded, he opened the door and stepped inside. The faucet squeaked. Bathwater gushed into the tub. Curious, she scooped Nicholas into her arms and peeked her head inside. Tara couldn't help but notice how his tight jeans outlined his muscular thighs.

Logan sat on the edge of the tub with his palm under the running water. "Do you like very hot showers?"

"Why?" The question seemed overly personal. She had no intention of telling him she preferred a bath.

Reaching to his shirt pocket, he jerked out her list. "Your instructions say to lower the setting on your hot water heater to one hundred and twenty degrees so it will be less likely to cause burns. Or, I can place knob covers over the bathtub fixtures and make it difficult for little fingers to change the water temperature.''

"I would never leave Nicholas alone in the tub!" she shot back.

He arched his brows. "Why are you so defensive?"

"Am I?" she blurted, aware of her trembling voice.

"You act like I'm accusing you of negligence. You're the one who gave me the list, remember?"

Shifting Nicholas to her hip and trying to project an air of calm and self-confidence, she plucked the list of instructions from his hand.

He chuckled and looked at her oddly. "You haven't read them?"

Ignoring his amusement, she read aloud. "Install nonslip rubber strips in the tub and a lock on the medicine cabinet and the commode? Do you know how to—"

"I build houses from the foundation up." He drilled her with an arrogant stare. "I can handle a few safety latches on the john."

He returned his attention to his work, a grim look darkening his face. She guessed he'd rather be elbow deep in concrete and plaster than adjusting the water temperature for her bath. She suppressed a grin.

He leaned against the tile wall and reached into the closet that held the hot water heater, his shirt stretching across his chest. After adjusting the thermostat, he dried the tub with a towel and applied rubber safety strips. Lost in thought, she stared at his capable hands, liking the way he held his tools in his large, callused palms. For once, not even Nicholas squirmed.

When Logan glanced up and caught her watching him, he gave her a look hot enough to melt a polar ice cap. Heat flushed her cheeks.

"I'll leave you to your work. If you need me, I'll be in the den with Nicholas."

He must think she'd never seen a man before, but it worried her that she couldn't stop her peculiar behavior or her odd reactions to having him in the house. Since she had no intention of repeating her mistakes, she retreated to the den to put her spinning thoughts in order.

In the family room, she concentrated on Nicholas, and in the hour that followed, regained her composure. Logan Stone needn't disturb the new life she intended to create, a life without a man. She'd spent too much time trying to be someone else in an effort to please Joe. Now that he was gone, she'd reverted to using her maiden name, and she could do what she wanted. No man would ever again take her confidence away.

Logan returned to the kitchen, so she delayed Nicholas's snack. She sat on the floor of the den stacking his blocks and letting him knock them down.

As Logan drilled and hammered the cabinet doors, the sounds enticed Nicholas. Curious, her son kept crawling toward the kitchen, and repeatedly, she pulled him back, trying to interest him in his toys. The more she thwarted him, the more determined he became.

Ignoring his plastic bulldozer, Nicholas pulled himself upright on a coffee table and pointed to the kitchen. "Eat."

"Good boy! You said a new word."

Nicholas bounced up and down with every syllable. "Eat. Eat. Eat."

She laughed. "Are you hungry?"

Nicholas let go of the table and balanced on his feet for a moment. "Uh-oh." He plopped onto his bottom, then, undeterred by the small mishap, he crawled to her.

She picked him up, perturbed by her own reluctance to enter the kitchen with Logan there. No man would ever again make her uncomfortable in her own home. "Come on, let's find you a snack. How about milk and some animal crackers?"

She entered the room as if invading enemy territory and averted her eyes from Logan, who was applying knob covers to prevent Nicholas from turning on the oven. After strapping her son in his high chair, she poured milk into his covered cup and gave him four animal cookies. "Look, sweetheart, a camel—your favorite."

"I prefer the lions." Logan wore a deadpan expression.

"Why is that?"

"For all their fierce roaring, they're only big pussycats."

"You sound like you speak from personal experience."

A shadow crossed his face, a suggestion of a dark emotion she couldn't begin to interpret. Then his face cleared and he spoke easily. "I used to be a stuntman. I've worked with a few big cats."

Reaching into the cookie box, she rummaged for a lion and offered it to Logan. "For you."

Nicholas clapped his pudgy hands. "Eat."

Logan accepted the tiny cookie, popped it into his mouth and limped over to Nicholas's chair. When he stuck out his tongue with the unchewed lion lying flat, Nicholas laughed in delight.

Odd how he acted wary with her, but let down his guard around Nicholas. With his knack for play, he'd make an excellent father.

The shrill of the phone jerked Tara from her wandering thoughts, and with instantly skyrocketing hopes she picked up the receiver. She'd sent résumés to every realty company in town. With luck, one of them might lead to an interview. From there, she'd have to wing it and hope no one checked her references, her family, her past. But even if she resorted to waiting on tables, she had to find work soon. She needed the money.

"Hello."

Grabbing a pen from a kitchen drawer, she listened to Mr. Bittner while scribbling the address and phone number he gave her on the top of an unpacked carton.

"I'll be there at four," she agreed, then hung up the phone with a grin.

"Good news?" Logan asked.

A warm surge of anticipation flowed through her. "One of Equity Real Estates's salespeople just eloped and left them shorthanded, so they want to interview me right away. The best part is that they guarantee a salary against commission."

And they needed someone now, which meant they wouldn't have time to do a thorough background check.

Logan glanced out the window. "The storm is about to break. You shouldn't drive in this weather."

"I won't be gone long."

"I'll lock the door behind me when I leave," he offered, obviously assuming she'd take Nicholas with her.

She hoped she wouldn't have to have the interview while juggling a baby on her lap. She opened a kitchen drawer and pulled out her phone book, glad she'd had the foresight to line up the baby-sitter Barbara recommended.

Penny Scott lived four doors down the block, and yesterday, Tara had questioned her thoroughly. Cheerful and enthusiastic, Penny seemed capable and anxious to please. While her cheerleader smile alone might have won Tara's confidence, the fact Barbara had known the Scotts for years made the decision even easier. At nineteen, and only four years younger than Tara, Penny would have been in college if she hadn't stayed home to look after her grandmother.

Tara picked up the receiver and dialed the number. With luck, Penny would be available on such short notice. She listened to three rings with a sinking heart.

Finally, a voice on the other end said a perky "Hello."

"Penny? This is Tara Larson. Could you baby-sit for the next hour or so?"

"Oh, hi, Ms. Larson. No problem. Grandma's going out to dinner with friends. I'll be right over."

Hanging up the phone, Tara checked her watch. Just enough time for a quick shower.

Logan lifted his head from the interior of a kitchen cabinet. "I couldn't help overhearing. Penny Scott is a great kid."

"You know her?"

"Her brother, Mike, and I were friends in high school. He's a cop now. Too bad she never went on to college." Logan echoed her own sentiments. "As I recall, she graduated first in her class."

Tara scooped Nicholas out of his chair and hurried down the hall. Logan's words helped ease any reservations about leaving Nicholas with someone she didn't know well.

After she changed another diaper, she kissed Nicholas's forehead and put him in his playpen. She shucked off her jeans and sweater, showered, then donned a white silk blouse, black wool skirt and matching jacket. While she applied makeup and quickly brushed her hair, her pulse quickened in anticipation of success. For once, everything seemed to be in her favor.

When Penny arrived, Tara led her back to Nicholas in the bedroom. "You won't have any trouble. He rarely cries. He's a terrific baby."

"I'll take good care of him," Penny promised.

"Equity's number is by the phone in the kitchen. I'll only be fifteen minutes away, so call if you need anything."

A drill whirred in the kitchen, reminding Tara that in her haste she'd almost neglected to tell Penny there was a man in the house. "Oh, Logan Stone is doing some work in the kitchen."

Penny, her auburn ponytail bouncing, picked Nicholas up from the crib, handed him his dinosaur and swung him onto her hip. "Logan Stone! I haven't seen him since he got back from California. I'll have to give him Mike's new number."

Tara looked at her watch and hesitated. Should she go over Nicholas's routine with Penny again?

From the kitchen, Logan waved goodbye. The baby-sitter smiled and patted her arm. "Go. The sooner you leave, the sooner you'll get back. You want to beat the storm, don't you?"

Tara kissed Nicholas goodbye, grabbed her good coat from the closet and slipped on her shoes. She walked down the long hall, her heels beating a firm staccato. Her future depended on landing this job, and she didn't want to waste another minute.

She rushed out onto the porch, shut the door behind her and stopped, her feet rooted to the welcome mat. During the last ten months, she hadn't once been separated from her son.

She took a step forward, dug her gloves out of her purse and paused again. An icy shiver crawled down her spine. And it had nothing to do with the weather.

Chapter Two

Penny played with Nicholas while Logan installed a safety latch on the microwave. Against his will, his thoughts returned to Tara.

It wasn't just her wary blue eyes that had jolted him out of his normal indifference to women, or the way her bottom swayed beneath her sensible skirt, or even the white silk of her blouse peeking through the triangle of her fitted jacket. While he couldn't help noticing the engaging slant of her high cheekbones, her trim waist and long legs, he couldn't ignore her strange combination of strength and vulnerability, attributes she probably used to her advantage.

Like many beautiful women, she no doubt exploited her looks to hide secrets. She was definitely concealing something. Why else would she be so defensive when he asked such simple questions?

He resented the memories she evoked, hated it when he found himself rehashing the worst moments of his life. His former fiancée had been just as attractive as Tara Larson, and she'd had her secrets, too.

With the memory of Allison, he savagely twisted a screw. Pretty, passionate, deceitful. Allison could have won an Academy Award for her acting ability. She'd used him to further her career, and fool that he'd been, he'd never suspected she'd had ulterior motives. The pain of her betrayal had long since disappeared, leaving in its place a healthy dose of cynicism toward all women. His knuckles tightened his clasp on the screwdriver. His attitude might not be rational, but his gut couldn't let it go.

He had stepped away from the microwave and started on the dishwasher when a persistent knocking on the front door broke his thoughts. Now what? Walking down the hall, he almost bumped into Penny, who held Nicholas on her hip.

"I'll get it." They both spoke at the same time.

"Mama?" Nicholas asked.

"She'll be back soon, sweetie." Penny smoothed back his wispy bangs, watching as Logan opened the door.

Big flakes of snow whisked into the foyer, melting as soon as they touched the brick floor. A young girl, about eight years old, Logan guessed, stood on the stoop, hands thrust in her pockets. "Penny, you got to come quick."

"What's wrong?"

"Your grandma fell on the sidewalk. My mom thinks she's hurt bad."

"Oh, my God!" Penny gasped.

She spun to face Logan. "You'll have to watch Nicholas until I get back. I can't take him out in this weather."

Before he could protest, she thrust Nicholas into his hands. His stomach plummeted as if he'd just jumped off a ten-story building without an air bag to break his fall. "I can't...I don't know how..."

Penny shoved one arm into her coat, stepped into her boots and raced out the door, shouting over her shoulder, "You'll be fine. I'll be back as soon as I can."

Nicholas burst into tears.

"I'm with you, pal." Logan awkwardly brought the child against his chest and closed the door to shut out the bitter wind.

Now what? Tossing a ball to a few kids between action scenes on a set hardly qualified him to take care of a baby. Damn! Why hadn't he insisted Penny take the child with her?

Nicholas kicked his tiny feet and shoved against Logan's chest. "Mama. Mama. Want Mama."

Logan feared he was holding Nicholas too firmly, but if he loosened his grip, he'd drop the wiggling child, who had more strength in his short little body than he'd have believed possible. Shifting Nicholas higher on his shoulder, Logan headed straight for the kitchen and the nearest telephone. He'd call Tara, and she'd come home. He'd heard her tell Penny she was only fifteen minutes away. With the snow coming down, she might take longer, but what could go wrong in twenty minutes?

Nicholas screwed up his face and screamed. Tears rained from his eyes, and his face turned cherry red. The noise grated on Logan's ears, his jaw tensed, and he jiggled the baby.

"Stop crying," he said in desperation.

To his surprise, his gruff words calmed the child. Nicholas hiccuped once, then settled down.

"Mama."

"I'm calling her right now." He placed Nicholas on a kitchen chair.

The baby slapped his palm on the table. "Eat."

As he searched for the phone number, the storm blocked the sun, darkening the room. A brief glance outside revealed the wind sweeping the snow ever faster and thicker. Tara had no business going out in such weather. Why couldn't women temper their ambition with common sense?

He turned on the kitchen light and found the number Tara had left. Clutching the piece of paper like a lifeline, he squinted at the writing. "Here it is. Equity Real Estate."

As he reached for the phone, out of the corner of his eye he caught sight of Nicholas climbing across the kitchen table toward the box of animal crackers Tara had left there. He dropped the phone and lunged for the child. "No, Nicholas."

"Eat."

When Logan grabbed the back of his pants and hoisted him off the table, the little scamp turned his head, grinned engagingly and burst out with a bubbly laugh. Logan jiggled him for a moment before tucking him safely in the crook of his arm. Sweat beaded his brow. He simply wasn't cut out for this kind of work. Nowhere on his business card did it read, Logan Stone, Baby-sitter.

Calm down.

He was a grown man. Surely he could watch one small child for less than an hour. He looked longingly at the phone, but didn't dare let Nicholas loose while he attempted the call. Instead, he put the baby in his high chair and strapped him in.

So far, so good. The child's feet had slipped into the correct holes like they were supposed to, and he was busy eating cookies. At least he'd stopped crying.

Logan picked up the phone, and when he didn't hear a dial tone, shook the receiver. Had it broken when he dropped it? He inspected it, then put it to his ear again, but it was no use. The phone was dead.

Hanging up, he pushed the high chair down the hall into the back bedroom. He wouldn't pick up the kid again if he could avoid it, and Nicholas seemed happy enough cramming crackers into his mouth. He didn't even chew the damn things.

An odd sound gurgled from the baby's mouth.

Logan stopped pushing the chair, crouched as low as his bad knee allowed, and observed the child with suspicion. The little devil's cheeks looked like a balloon ready to pop. He could choke!

Grasping the baby's mouth, he gently pried it open. Nicholas screamed, spitting half-eaten animal crackers all over himself, all over Logan, and all over the wall.

Laughing, the kid held up his arms as if asking Logan to pick him up. "Yuk."

Logan sighed. "You have a way of stating the obvious, pal."

"Eat."

"No more eat." Logan raked a hand through his hair, smearing soggy cookie crumbs onto his face. He ignored the sticky mess sliding down his cheek.

"We're going to call your mama."

"Mama. Mama." Nicholas bounced in his chair, looking past him for Tara.

Even he should know better than to say her name. When Tara finally showed, he didn't know who would be more relieved to see her, Nicholas or him. He was lucky the kid hadn't started screaming again at the mention of her name. But Nicholas had found a partially eaten cookie on his tray and was busy shoving it into his mouth.

Overcoming his reluctance to hold the baby, he untied Nicholas from the high chair, stopped in the hallway bathroom and made an attempt to wipe his grubby face clean. Nicholas wriggled wildly, and Logan gave up. A few crumbs wouldn't hurt him.

"Let's go, pal."

Nicholas clapped his chubby hands together, spattering more cookie crumbs. "Go. Go."

Logan spied the playpen, and his trepidation eased. The baby would be safe there while he called Tara. He was about to snap on the light when Nicholas yawned and his body relaxed and cuddled against him. Perhaps the child would sleep if he left the room dark. Could he possibly get that lucky?

As he placed Nicholas on the plastic cushion amid his toys without a protest, a great weight lifted from Logan's chest. He'd expected a cry when he left, but the child snuggled with his blanket and sucked his finger.

Logan strode into the master bedroom, picked up the phone, and cursed. Still no dial tone. The storm must have knocked out the lines.

He walked to the window, listening for a baby's cry, but the house remained silent. Drawing the curtain aside, he stared out into the worst storm of the winter. He could barely see lights in the neighbors' houses through the now-billowing snow.

With the weather like this, Tara should have had the sense to return early, but he knew better than to count on a woman to do anything so logical. He hadn't survived three sisters without learning something about the unpredictable ways the female mind worked.

While Nicholas slept, Logan returned to the hallway and cleaned the cookie mess off the wood floor before resuming work in the bathroom. He turned on his radio for news and went back to installing the safety latches. A weather bulletin announced that eight inches of snow had already fallen and predicted another two feet in the next few hours. The news finally turned from the snowstorm to a mother making a plea for help in finding her child who'd been kidnapped from her home.

Kidnappers. As a precaution, Tara should have dead bolts on every door. He made a mental note to buy the hardware and install them tomorrow.

At the increasing howl of the storm, Nicholas cried out.

Now what? Logan dashed for the child's room, ignoring the pain in his bad knee.

Opening the door, he paused on the threshold of the dark room and fumbled for the light switch. Out of the corner of his eye, he caught a glint in the shadows, heard a stifled breath and detected a fleet movement toward the door. He lunged with his arms wide.

And smashed into someone holding Nicholas.

"Mama."

Logan stumbled backward, snatching the baby from the other's grip. The intruder shoved them, and Logan, already off balance, twisted to protect the child as they tumbled to the floor. He landed hard on his shoulder. At the impact, his vision clouded, and he gritted his teeth against the fiery agony, fighting to remain conscious and maintain his hold on Nicholas. Pains shunted through him while the intruder escaped down the hall. The back door slammed.

Nicholas. He had to keep him safe. Whoever had tried to take him could come back.

The child whimpered softly on his chest, and Logan held him with his good arm. Rolling to his side, he groaned.

Damn it to hell! He'd dislocated his shoulder again. It had happened before during high school gymnastic practice when he'd careened off a trampoline, and again years later, when he'd slid across concrete during a chase scene. One sharp thump would snap the shoulder back into place, but the agony might knock him senseless. He couldn't risk it with a baby to protect.

He moaned, unable to hold back the pain. It would be so easy to give in and slip away into blackness. No, the baby needed him. Nicholas lifted his head, and Logan awkwardly patted his back. He sucked in his breath and gathered his strength, steeling himself against the agony.

Moving inch by torturous inch to a sitting position where the wall supported his back, he held on to one thought. He couldn't let anyone harm this child.

Sharp colors burst inside his head. He slumped. And he sank toward a comforting darkness.

Don't go to sleep. Fight.

He shook his head to clear it. Stay awake. Nicholas. Odd, the kid seemed to be sleeping. Logan breathed in shallow gasps, trying to hold absolutely still.

He...had...to...hold...on...

TARA DROVE THROUGH the snow, pleased the storm had cut her interview short. Mr. Bittner had never gotten around to asking about her credentials. Instead, he'd spoken about dedication, honesty and loyalty to the firm, and complained about the woman who'd left him shorthanded with only a one-day notice. Tara had listened politely, and he'd seemed impressed with the determination she showed, coming out for the job interview during this weather.

She turned on her wipers and grinned despite the poor visibility. She had a job! One she'd gotten all by herself. Moving to a town where no one knew her had been the first step to independence. Finding work, her second. A small thrill shot up her spine. Success felt great!

The trip home was taking three times longer than she anticipated. When her headlights could no longer pierce the snow, she leaned forward, neck and shoulders tensed, peering through the windshield and steering with care over the treacherous streets.

The main road had been plowed and salted, but when she turned into her neighborhood, snowdrifts blocked her path. As she eased her car forward, it skidded, and the wheels spun without traction.

For a moment she didn't breathe. Then slowly, she regained control of her car, pulled over to the curb and shut off the engine. After several calming breaths, she decided to walk the last two blocks. When she opened the car door, gusting wind almost ripped it from her hand, and she had to lean her weight into the door to close it.

Within seconds her thin shoes were soaked, and beneath her skirt, the cold stung her legs. She suddenly remembered Joe had always kept a raincoat in the trunk. Trudging to the rear of the car, she found the black slicker and put it on, thankful for the hood that protected her face from the cutting wind.

Keeping her head down, she plodded through the deepening snow, lumbered through the drifts and peered ahead for a familiar landmark. Ah, there was her house. By the time she reached the side door, she was out of breath.

She used her key to let herself in. "Hello. Penny?"

No answer. She walked through the den, past the kitchen, flipping on lights. They must be in the bedroom.

As she approached the hall, she heard the bathwater running. So, Penny was giving Nicholas a bath. She pictured him splashing happily, pushing his floating toy boat and making waves.

She turned on the light and hurried down the hall toward her room. She'd remove her sodden hose and hang up the wet raincoat in the shower before joining Penny and Nicholas. When her wet feet slid on the wooden floor, she looked down to regain her balance.

Abruptly the bathroom door opened, and someone careered into her. Her head jerked up, and her arms flailed. A stranger with dark, dangerous eyes attacked, his arms encircling her in a vicelike grip that forced the air from her lungs.

A low growl of rage escaped his lips. "You can't have him."

For an instant, they clung together and fought for balance. "Logan?"

Recognition flickered in his eyes.

But the force of the impact of his hard body colliding with hers knocked her off balance. Her feet slid out from under her, and she fell, knocking Logan backward. He groaned when his back slammed into the floor and she landed on his broad chest.

Tangled in the folds of her loose coat, she lifted her gaze to him. His sunken cheeks had turned pasty gray, his lips pinched tight, and his face was contorted in soundless agony.

"Where're you hurt?" she asked.

He didn't move. Didn't answer. Lord, he looked as if he was going to pass out. Blood trickled from the corner of his mouth. The pupils of his black eyes were dilated, and his gaze appeared unfocused.

"It's Tara. Where's—"

"Under . . . sink."

His dazed expression cleared for an instant. Beneath her, his big body shuddered. His head wrenched up, and he gasped with the effort. His lids fluttered closed, and his hard muscles lost their rigidity.

What was going on? She lurched to her feet. Where was the baby-sitter? And Nicholas? Where was her child? "Nicholas? Penny?"

Silence loomed around Tara like a heavy mist. Terror gripped her, and she tried to hold on to her fragile control. She staggered through the open bathroom door, turned off the running water and checked the tub for her son.

Empty.

She choked back a cry. Her heart pounded so hard that her ears roared. She ran, slipping and sliding, to the baby's room, turned on the light and looked in the crib.

Empty—except for his green dinosaur.

Horror clawed her throat. Think. She had to be strong for her son. Every moment might be critical. What had Logan said? Something about a sink.

She sprinted to the kitchen and flicked on the light, then tugged on the cabinet door, but the safety lock Logan had installed stopped it from opening. Sobbing, she searched for the childproof latch and yanked the door open.

Empty!

As she slumped in despair, icy fear sank into her every pore. Joe had always told her she would never be strong enough when her son needed her, and the memory of his words rose up to haunt her in her frantic search. His handsome face had sneered as he listed her inadequacies in that cold, logical way she hated.

The knowledge of what she'd almost become while she tried to please her husband twisted inside her. Weak, wimpy, worthless. He'd thought her silent and defeated. But she had never believed him then. And she wouldn't give up now.

Springing to her feet, she returned to the bathroom and reached under the sink for the cabinet knobs. Half in anticipation, half in dread, she flung the doors open.

Nicholas slept peacefully. With a towel pillowed under his head and cookie crumbs around his mouth, he smiled in his sleep. He was safe. Safe.

Thank, God! She sagged to the floor and sobbed with relief.

As she gathered him into her trembling arms, he didn't stir. Drawing his warmth against her chest, she fought the urge to squeeze him too tightly.

Her gaze rested on Logan, out cold on the hardwood floor. What the hell had happened while she'd been gone? Where was Penny? Why was Logan still here?

She should phone the police and have them send an ambulance. Then she remembered the phones had been out when she'd tried to call from the real estate office.

She and her child were alone in the house with this stranger.

As she held Nicholas and stared at Logan, she relived the moment she'd bumped into him. Her head had been down. She'd caught one glimpse of his savage eyes before he'd seized her. With his violence like a volcano on the verge of erupting, he'd been ready to do battle.

Her brow furrowed. Should she fear him?

He now lay helpless on the floor by her feet, but she recalled the strength in his arms, the power in his chest, the ferocity in his eyes. Even injured, this man could be dangerous.

Holding Nicholas safe, she considered the situation, ticking off points in his favor. One, Logan had stopped his attack the moment he recognized her. Two, he was her best friend's cousin. And three, even through his pain, he'd told her where he'd put the baby. He couldn't have meant them any harm.

But Logan had hidden her son. Was he trying to protect him? From what? Had he been hurt protecting Nicholas? If she could revive him, he'd tell her what had happened, but her first concern was her child.

She started to take Nicholas to his crib, then stopped. She shouldn't leave Nicholas alone—not even for a moment.

Returning to the kitchen, she tore into one of the packed boxes and retrieved a child carrier she rarely used because Nicholas had grown so. But he still fit into the sling. She strapped the sleeping child to her and was comforted by his closeness.

Once she'd positioned the baby against her chest, she lifted the phone off the hook and held it to her ear. Still dead.

She couldn't call for help, and she couldn't take Nicholas out in this weather. Even if she plodded through the snow to her car, driving to reach help for the man stretched unconscious on her hall floor was too dangerous.

How badly was Logan hurt? Maybe he'd regain consciousness soon. She needed to check his injuries more carefully, but first, for protection against intruders, she lifted a wine bottle, a housewarming gift from Barbara, from the counter and returned to Logan.

He hadn't moved. She placed the bottle within easy reach and ran her hands through his thick hair, searching for a cut, a knot, some indication of his injury. Her gaze lingered on his lush hair, square jaw

and too-handsome face. She squirmed, remembering
how she hadn't had the courage to meet his black gaze.
Just having him in the house caused her heart to hammer oddly in her chest. But she couldn't let herself be
attracted to him. She didn't want to be close to any
man.

He had one of those take-charge personalities, pro-
jecting an insistence to do things his way. Were those
traits typical of all big handsome men? Joe had had
that same need to take charge, so had her father-in-
law, and now Logan Stone. Her marriage had few
problems until she realized she didn't want Joe making all the decisions.

A muscle in Logan's neck twitched, drawing her
from her thoughts. As his lids snapped open, she
jerked her hands from his hair as if she'd been scalded.

He blinked several times, his long lashes shadow-
ing his cheeks, a tinge of pink replacing the ashen
color of his skin. "What . . . happened?"

"That was one of my questions. Where's the baby-
sitter?"

"Gone." He caught her arm in a firm grip. "Is the
baby okay?"

She narrowed her eyes, knowing she couldn't break
free of the fingers clenching her arm. "Why shouldn't
he be?"

"I thought . . . you were the kidnapper." His mouth
firmed in a sardonic twist.

Kidnapper! Her stomach spasmed in the tightening
grip of panic. Icy terror crawled over her nape. She
reached for the wine bottle and clenched it with sweaty

palms, taking little comfort in its weight. "Someone tried to take Nicholas? Who? Why?"

Logan groaned, and his lids fluttered closed. She couldn't count on him remaining conscious, nor could she count on more of his help. Her pulse pounded.

She and Nicholas were alone, and someone was after her son.

Calm down. Think. Head injuries were tricky, and while she shouldn't remove Logan from his position on the floor she could find him a blanket to keep warm.

Urgency rushed through her, but she hesitated. If the kidnapper returned, she'd have to protect all of them, and a wine bottle wasn't much of a weapon.

Thump. The back door slammed. She clutched Nicholas with one hand and gripped her makeshift weapon in the other.

What was that? She listened. A cold sweat broke out on her forehead.

Was someone else in the house?

Chapter Three

When the door slammed, Logan's shoulders jerked. His eyes opened and slowly focused.

Tara leaned over him and kept her voice low. "I think someone's in the house."

Thud.

Signaling him to silence with her finger to her lips, she held her breath, straining for the sound of footsteps on the hardwood floor. Only a cold draft of air whispered through the hall.

Logan didn't make a noise but spent his energy wriggling closer to the bathroom wall. Perspiration beaded his lip.

What should she do? "Maybe I should go for help."

His voice was raw, insistent. "No. You'll be safer with me."

"I could make a run for it."

"And the kidnapper could be waiting outside."

He sounded so sure of himself, and yet he could barely crawl. The pain obviously hadn't shaken his confidence. And the thought of taking Nicholas into the dark, into the blizzard with nothing to protect her but a wine bottle, settled the matter. There could be danger inside or out. At least here they were warm.

The door slammed and thudded. Then slammed again. Although she attempted to control her fright, Logan must have seen her tighten her grip on Nicholas.

"It's probably just the wind slamming the back door."

At his reasonable explanation for the noise, the stiffness in her shoulders and back eased, and her breathing slowed to normal. No one intent on deceit would make such an incessant racket. And if someone was in the house, the intruder most likely would have confronted them by now—or so she hoped. With her immediate fear lessening, concern for Logan rose to the forefront. "You should stay still."

Ignoring her suggestion, he advanced another three inches along the floor. "If I can reach the doorway, I'll pull myself up."

She shoved a stray lock of hair from her eyes and examined the cord of muscles straining his neck, his taut cheeks and his clenched jaw. "You look like hell."

"And your bedside manner leaves something to be desired."

She sighed, knowing he was right. She should be offering comfort, but his refusal to lie still and his foolhardy confidence irritated her. But this was no time for petty concerns, he could have internal injuries, and she knew very little first aid. "Would you like a bag of ice? An aspirin?"

"How about a shoulder replacement." He raised his hand across his chest to his shoulder, rubbed the muscles and winced. When he noticed her skepticism, he tried to reassure her. "It's getting better."

"What happened to Penny? Why did you put Nicholas under the sink?"

"Could we continue this conversation in the den? Preferably from a chair?" His gaze locked on the wine bottle. "And if you're not going to club me, I could use a drink."

She rocked back on her heels to consider him. He confused her. Why wasn't he content to lie still? His determination reminded her of when he'd lunged from the bathroom, thinking she was a kidnapper. She'd never forget the wildness in his eyes. But now if she read the gleam of purpose in his gaze correctly, he intended to protect her and Nicholas.

"I'll pull myself to a sitting position." His good hand clamped around the molding of the bathroom door. "Are you going to stand there and watch, or help?"

"What do you want me to do?"

His pale lips clenched into a grimace fiercer than the winter storm. "If I pass out, keep my head from slamming to the floor again."

"Maybe you shouldn't—"

He groaned and pulled himself up. His face stiffened, every muscle rigid. As he shut his eyes and breathed short pants, she remained ready to ease him to the floor if he fell.

Absently, he wiped the blood from his mouth with the back of his wrist, then drew his knees to his chest. He held out his good hand to her. "Pull me to my feet."

She shook her head, admiring his tenacity. But was the additional pain he suffered worth the effort? "I could get you a pillow. You could—"

"Fine. I'll do it myself."

When she still hesitated to step closer and take his hand, he tilted his head back and looked up at her. "Are you afraid to touch me?"

Yes. "Of course not!" Except for his handshake, no man had touched her since the day Joe died. At Joe's funeral, she'd refused to let even her father-in-law put his arm around her, and now Logan held out his hand, having no idea how much his touch affected her. Perhaps she'd imagined the tingling sensation she'd felt when they'd first met. There was only one way to find out.

She reached out, and his large fingers engulfed hers, again catching her unprepared. His warmth, calluses and undeniable strength sent a burst of heat racing up her arm.

He gave her fingers a gentle squeeze. "Ready?"

Nodding, she leaned back to counterbalance his weight while he gathered his feet under him and pulled himself upright. The color he'd regained disappeared, and his skin turned ashen. His jaw clenched in pain, and he staggered. She shifted forward, compensating for Nicholas against her chest.

She pulled Logan's good arm over her shoulder to steady him. "There's no hurry. Take your time."

He leaned heavily against her, and she inhaled his manly scent, an attractive mixture of sawdust and soap with a trace of leather. As his arm circled her shoulders for support, she bent into the rock-hard tension of his muscles.

Logan had been successfully seated in the chair in the den a good five minutes before her pulse returned to normal. Touching him had been like snuggling under a cozy blanket on a chilly winter night. The thought unsettled her, and she didn't look at him for a moment or two, but when she gathered her courage and turned his way, his head rested against the back of the lounge chair with his eyes closed.

Barbara hadn't lied when she'd said her cousin was strong, dark and silent. The sunny yellow room framed his dark good looks, but it wasn't his rugged handsomeness she'd responded to. Although she wouldn't easily forget how his solid muscles had pressed against her, she'd forever remember how he'd protected her son while in pain. Joe would have been complaining about his discomfort and accusing her of causing it. But Logan hadn't cast one word of blame.

He hadn't told her what had happened, either.

Nicholas yawned, and she patted his back. With luck, he'd go back to sleep.

As her gaze roved over Logan's long eyelashes, straight nose and rugged jaw, his eyes opened. Raising his hand to the back of his head, he gingerly rubbed his neck while he held her glance.

Lord, his stare went straight to her soul. "Are you okay? Perhaps you should lie down."

"Don't you dare move me another inch," he said with a strained grimace. "I can see two of you, and you both look beautifully concerned."

It had been too long since she'd received a compliment. She warmed to his words and grinned. "Would you like an aspirin for the pain?"

He waved his hand dismissively. "What pain? How about some wine?"

She took two wineglasses from the sideboard. "The bottle's one of those twist-off corks, but I can't open it."

She waited for him to say something sarcastic and make fun of her lack of strength. Old habits died hard. When he remained silent, she chanced a glance at him.

He beckoned her closer. "Perhaps we can do this together. Hold the bottle tight, and I'll remove the cork."

His suggestion startled her because it was so sensible, so normal. She could get used to being treated like a person again.

Placing the wine on his knee, she reached around Nicholas and held the bottom of the bottle tightly. With his good hand, Logan gripped the cork. She braced herself against one huge tug, but again he surprised her, twisting the cork between his thumb and forefinger, patiently working it loose.

She poured him a glass, took one for herself, then sat opposite him on the couch, cradling Nicholas on her lap. Savoring the flavor, she watched Logan take a sip.

"Well?" She couldn't contain her curiosity another moment. "What happened?"

"First, go lock every door and check the windows."

"Why? The intruder is long gone."

"Just do it."

His voice hit her like a whip, and she jumped, spilling her wine. Grabbing a napkin from a tray, she blotted the tiny spot on the couch. "I'll get some cold water. It should come right out."

"I'm sure it will." He cleared his throat and she looked up. "Sorry. I shouldn't have snapped at you."

He'd apologized instead of berating her for questioning him or spilling the wine. This man was nothing like Joe, but she couldn't stop responding as if he were. Joe had never laid a hand on her, but she'd conditioned herself to try to please him, and she'd never understood why all her efforts had failed.

Never again, she vowed for the thousandth time. Never again would she place herself in the vulnerable position of tying her self-respect to a man's approval. Over the last ten months she'd discovered the power of pleasing only herself, but she was dismayed to learn the ingrained habits refused to die.

She set down her glass, stood and placed her hands on her hips. "After I've checked the locks, you're going to tell me what happened."

As he raised his glass in a salute and nodded, his face was cool, handsome, expressionless.

Carrying Nicholas, she hurried away to the foyer. It had been so easy to make a demand. So why were her insides trembling, her stomach twisted like a pretzel?

She checked the front door and patted Nicholas's back, as if the soothing motions could ease the tension inside her. Both the dead bolt and the regular lock were secure. Next she entered the kitchen in the remodeled end of the house. She walked across the gleaming tile to the sliding glass door by the patio, checking the two-by-four still in its track.

The wooden door by the stoop stood ajar. Snow whisked through the kitchen door, but it wasn't the frigid air that caused her breath to freeze in her throat. Outside, newly fallen snow partially filled tracks that led from her stoop into the darkness of the woods beyond.

She slammed the door and locked it. Before returning to Logan in the den, she made a sweep of the house until she was satisfied every window was secure.

Stopping in her bedroom, she removed the papoose with Nicholas inside, and he never awakened when she placed him on her bed. She took off her wet stockings and skirt, donned a pair of jeans, then slipped the papoose's straps over her shoulders.

Feigning composure, she returned to Logan. "You were right, the kitchen door was open."

Logan nodded, as if he'd expected her words. "Why don't you have a seat and finish your wine?"

She didn't want a drink, she wanted answers, but she returned to her place on the couch and folded her legs beneath her. She tried to keep impatience from her voice. "I saw tracks. Why did Penny leave?"

"Her grandmother had an accident."

Tara made a mental note to call Penny and see if her grandmother was okay. "Did Penny go out the back door?"

He shook his head. "I locked the *front* door behind her."

"You're sure?"

Logan stared out the window, sitting still and brooding. "Yes."

"Go on." She leaned forward, twirling the stem of her wineglass.

"Nicholas ate a few cookies, then I put him in his playpen and returned to finish the bathroom latches.

When he cried out, I ran to the bedroom. Someone was there and had taken him from his playpen. I grabbed Nicholas and fell in the process.''

"*He* seems fine." She'd already run her hands over every inch of her son, who didn't have so much as a bruise.

"I fell on my back and cushioned him. That's when I dislocated my shoulder."

Her stomach clenched at what might have happened if Logan had landed atop Nicholas instead of the other way around. "We should get you to a doctor."

He shrugged, then winced. "That won't be necessary. You already fixed it."

She eyed him suspiciously. "Really?"

"When we collided in the hall, it popped into place."

"Are you still seeing double?"

"I'm fine."

"Is that so?" She wasn't buying his self-diagnosis, thinking he was pushing the bravery bit too far.

"I've dislocated my shoulder before. It's already better. I feel up to sparring a few rounds."

"Yeah, right. You look ready to take on Mike Tyson." She sighed, realizing he would stop talking if she didn't keep prodding him with questions. "Why was Nicholas under the sink?"

He paused, then finally answered. "When you came into the house, I thought the kidnapper had returned. I hid Nicholas."

She tried to imagine him, hurt, alone in the dark with her baby. A few minutes ago, with the amount of pain he was in, he couldn't have made it to the den without her help. "How did you carry Nicholas all the way down the hall?"

"I scooted on my back with him on my chest."

When he'd jumped out at her, he'd been on his feet. "And how did you stand by yourself?"

"Steadied myself on the sink."

She scowled at his blasé tone. He must have been in agony. No wonder he'd passed out. "And the running bathwater?"

"A diversionary tactic. The noise covered my clumsy attack."

She didn't doubt his story. How could she after seeing the tracks in the snow? But how had he managed to get to his feet in so much pain? She recalled the wildness in his eyes. "You lunged into the hall before I passed the door."

"Bad timing. I couldn't hear your footsteps over the running water and had to guess your progress from the moment you turned on the light."

She suspected his timing was off from his injury, not her muffled footsteps. How could she ever thank him enough? He'd faced danger and endured pain to save her son. He was as wild as Barbara said. And thank God. He'd run into Nicholas's dark bedroom, not knowing whether the intruder possessed a weapon, all to protect her child.

She set down her wine and drew an afghan from the arm of the couch and tucked it around her son and her lap. "What did the kidnapper look like?"

Logan closed his eyes. "It was too dark."

"If Penny had been here, alone... If you hadn't..." She shuddered at the thought of what might have happened.

His frown deepened, and he spoke coldly, as if from experience. "Don't start thinking about might-have-beens. It'll drive you mad."

The terror she'd been trying to hold at bay suddenly gripped her. She sat on the couch and cradled her baby, rocking him, resisting the urge to hug him so tightly that he'd awaken. Her fingers smoothed his gossamer hair, two shades lighter than hers, and traced the silky skin of his neck in little circles.

If she'd been the one at home instead of Logan, she might not have protected Nicholas as well. Although she'd relished the time alone with her son these last months, right now she was grateful to have a man around the house.

Minutes passed before she could speak. "How can I thank you?"

His black eyes opened with a twinkle. "I thought you'd never ask. You could fix me dinner. I'm starved."

"How can you think of food when you're in so much pain?"

"My stomach growls and reminds me. No matter how badly I'm injured, I always wake up hungry."

She threw off the afghan and rose to her feet. "You've been hurt that often?"

"Naw. I just pretend, so pretty blue-eyed women will fix me dinner."

That was the second time he'd complimented her. A toasty warmth heated her stomach, easing the icy knot of fear. He was using his lighthearted teasing to take her mind off what had happened, and she appreciated his attempt.

"Dinner's coming right up." She headed for the kitchen, then hesitated. Turning back, she retrieved the afghan, floated it over him, then stuffed the edges down the side of the chair without touching or looking at him once.

As she leaned close, Logan inhaled her tangy-sweet scent. No woman had ever fussed over him so reluctantly. Was he a fool to consider Tara Larson different from every other woman he'd known? It was a good thing blond-haired, blue-eyed women with children weren't his type, because she intrigued him like no one he'd ever met.

Whenever she looked at her son, her face softened. For a moment, he wished she'd look at him with such concern and adoration in her eyes.

When she'd fallen on top of him, she'd been soft, yet fiery. His arms had closed around her automatically, and what a costly mistake that had been. He recalled the silky smoothness of her skin and mentally damned how easy it would be to want her.

He'd held his share of women, women tempted by his looks and intrigued by his hard-boiled attitude. But for the last two years, he'd never let passion rule him. He'd rarely dated the same woman for more than a week.

But when Tara had covered him with the afghan, he'd had an almost irresistible urge to draw her onto his lap, run his hands through her downy-soft hair, taste the fullness of her lips. He'd responded to her on a deep level that he hadn't known existed. Despite the lingering pain in his shoulder, he'd responded to her thoughtfulness in a most elemental way. Had she suspected he needed that blanket?

She'd slipped past his guard. But that just made her more clever, better able to get what she wanted before a man knew he was her target.

He told himself he wasn't interested. She reminded him too clearly of his past mistakes, mistakes he wasn't eager to repeat. He wouldn't pursue her, nor would he consider asking her out. No sense starting what he wouldn't finish.

"The phone's still down," she called from the kitchen.

He sighed. No way he could check on his sisters. Melissa could probably use some help with her horses. Delyn would never think to keep the water running, and a pipe would probably burst. And Eve would study so hard she'd forget to buy groceries. He remembered they had husbands to look after them now. Just thinking about his scatterbrained sisters made him tired.

He must have nodded off. When Tara returned with a tray, the sky was dark, but the snow hit the beams of the outside lights in a solid wave. The storm's fury was intensifying.

From his chair, he watched Nicholas in the kitchen, happily playing with some noodles on the tray of a portable swing. He'd wager a week's pay Tara hadn't yet let him out of her sight. Not that he blamed her after what had happened. He sniffed the vegetable soup, hot crusty bread and salad appreciatively.

"Smells good."

She placed the folding tray within his reach. "The forecasters don't expect the storm to clear until morning. And they say as soon as we dig out, another front is coming our way. Would you like me to turn on the news?''

''I'd rather you told me about yourself.''

Her brows lifted. ''There's nothing to tell.''

''You don't have any family in town?'' He asked just to make small talk.

As she pulled another folding tray close to the couch, she shook her head, and a cascade of shoulder-length blond hair hid her expression. ''My parents died a long time ago. I'm afraid there's only Nicholas and me. What about you?''

She was steering the conversation away from herself, but he wouldn't allow it. ''Do you know anyone who would want to take your child?''

Her fork paused on the way to her mouth. ''What makes you think the intruder wasn't a stranger?''

Her frightened look almost made him drop his inquiry. But unsettling her now would be better than putting her son at risk. ''How long ago did Nicholas's father die?''

''Ten months.''

''I'm sorry.''

''Don't be. I'm okay with it.''

His head jerked up at her callous admission. She'd said the words flatly, and he had no doubt she meant them. Why would she admit something like that? Curiosity burned inside him, but he refused to ask her more personal questions. He didn't want to hear her story, didn't want to be any more involved than he already was. Why should he be so surprised that this beautiful woman wasn't sorry her husband was dead? After all, he knew how treacherous some women could be.

And then, as if she'd just made the most ordinary statement in the world, she asked, "Would you like some more wine?"

"Not if I'm going to drive in this weather."

"My car didn't make it down this street."

"I have chains in my truck and four-wheel drive."

A myriad of emotions crossed her face. He expected her to protest his imminent departure, but she remained silent. While he could protect her if he stayed, clearly she didn't want him there any longer than necessary. But Nicholas could still be in danger.

Logan knew most missing children were abducted by a divorced parent or a family member. "What about grandparents?"

"Joe's father, Conrad Pemberton, is a very prominent man. While he might want to take my baby, he wouldn't resort to anything illegal."

As if to forestall more questions, she pushed her dinner aside, walked to the kitchen and turned the crank on Nicholas's swing.

When she returned, he continued his questions. "All right. Let's assume no one you know is after Nicholas. If a kidnapping ring is involved, how do you intend to protect your kid?"

"You think they might be back?"

"It's possible." Worry creased her brow, and he quickly added, "But probably not tonight. The weather would interfere with any getaway plans."

Her gaze darted to Nicholas and back to him, her eyes wide with distress. "What happens to the babies they steal?"

"I don't know. Infertile couples probably buy them on the black market. I've heard adoption can take years." Sensing she was hanging on to her composure by a thread, he kept to himself the possibility of child porno rings. There were a lot of sickos out there.

Tara walked to the fridge and opened the door. The bright yellow bulb highlighted her blond hair and emphasized her pale face. "Italian, Russian or blue cheese dressing?"

"Italian will be fine, thanks." Why was he being so polite? He had the notion she was waiting on him, anticipating his needs, instead of sharing their dinner. But her thoughts were clearly on her son, so the way she treated him was probably automatic. His impression strengthened when she started to pour the dressing on his salad instead of handing him the bottle.

"I can do that." He reached out and their fingers touched. She jerked back, and he almost dropped the bottle. When he looked up, a pretty blush heated her cheeks.

"Sorry." She rubbed her arms above her elbows. "I'm edgy."

"Understandable under the circumstances." And if she knew some of his more lustful thoughts, she'd probably run screaming. He ate some soup and gave her time to regain her composure. They dined in strained silence. But instead of appreciating a woman who didn't chatter, he suddenly wished she'd tell him more about herself.

At first she did more stirring of her soup than eating. Slowly a look of determination emerged on her face, and then she ate quietly, as if suddenly deciding she needed to keep up her strength. When they'd finished the meal, Logan wiped his lips with a napkin and tossed it onto the tray. He pushed back his plate and stood, mindful of his sore shoulder.

Her mouth dropped open. "Your shoulder?"

"It's better." He hesitated. "Is there a neighbor who could spend the night?"

"I just moved in. I don't know anyone except Penny."

Ask me to stay. Logan set aside his promise to remain distant. His concern for her safety overrode his wish to stay uninvolved. Although he didn't think anyone would risk coming out in this weather, if they did, she couldn't even call the police, and he inwardly cringed at the thought of leaving her—and little Nicholas—alone.

Tara collected the dishes on her tray. "I'll be fine." Her uncompromising tone left him no choice but to go.

"You're sure?"

"Even *you* don't think anyone will come back tonight."

But what would she do tomorrow and the day after that? Telling himself it wasn't his problem did nothing to alleviate his sense of responsibility. But he couldn't spend the rest of his life with her. His sense of protectiveness was kicking into overdrive, and as his sister, Eve, often told him, he needed to chill out.

He took an experimental step. "Check the phone once more, will you?"

Limping around the den, he tested his range of pain-free motion. His vision had cleared, and as long as he held his arm still, he'd manage. By the day after tomorrow, he'd be as good as new.

Tara returned, shaking her head. "No dial tone."

He'd expected that. "The first phone I see I'll call the police for you, and I'll drop by in the morning. Thanks for dinner."

"I owe you a lifetime of dinners after what you did."

Collecting all those dinners crossed his mind. What would it be like to know her better? Even now he ached to kiss her goodbye but refrained.

Picking up Nicholas and placing him on her hip, she followed him into the foyer. "Let me help you with your coat."

"Bye-bye."

"Yes, Nicholas. Logan is going bye-bye."

She didn't seem the least bit reluctant to let him walk out that door. As she helped him slip into his coat, she didn't touch him once. And when she handed him his cap, he could have sworn she deliberately turned it to avoid contact with his fingers. How could he be this attracted to a woman so obviously repelled by him? Or was she playing a game, using reverse psychology to win his interest?

With her eyes looking as cool and remote as yesterday's blue sky, he could tell nothing from her expression. He pulled his cap onto his head. "I'll see you in the morning. Lock up behind me."

"We'll be fine," she assured him.

She closed the door after him, and the click of the lock sounded hollow and empty in the suddenly lonely foyer. She'd considered asking him to stay, but remained too wary. If she'd had more time since Joe died, she might have been more comfortable with Logan in the house. But it was too soon.

She listened for the sound of the truck, but couldn't hear it above the howl of the wind. Looking out through the panes alongside the front door proved impossible since snow as thick as cotton balls stuck to the glass. She hoped the man who'd guarded her child made it home safe. Although she'd wanted him to go, once Logan had left, she admitted she'd felt safer with him there.

Nicholas fidgeted on her hip. He needed a bath, but it was already past his bedtime. Skipping playtime and his bath, she hurried him into his pajamas.

It wouldn't hurt for her son to sleep with her this once, she thought, pushing the cradle into her room. Just in case... She couldn't finish the thought.

She glanced down at her son, unwilling to miss another precious moment of their time together. Thanks to Joe's selfishness, she'd barely held Nicholas during his first month. Since then he'd grown so much. Already he was almost too long for the cradle's short mattress, but he settled in easily, tired from the excitement.

Smoothing back his hair, she kissed his forehead and shivered at how close she'd come to losing him. She started when branches scratched the icy windowpane.

The front doorbell rang.

Her heart dropped to her stomach. She wiped her hands on her jeans and hurried down the hall, trying to convince herself that a kidnapper would hardly ring the front bell. So why were her knees about to buckle?

A silhouette on the front porch cast an eerie shadow across the foyer. Should she refuse to answer? What if someone needed help in the storm? Taking a deep breath, she sought to maintain her composure and to keep her voice strong and fearless. "Who's there?"

Chapter Four

"Logan Stone."

Relief flowed through Tara. She opened the door, peeked through the crack, then unchained the latch. When Logan entered with a blast of cold air and took up most of the foyer, she retreated until her backside came up against a wall.

A hint of chagrin tempered his devilish tone. "Could you put me up for the night?"

No. She battled the desire to refuse aloud. But how could she deny Barbara's cousin, the man who'd saved her son? That would be unacceptable, intolerable, rude. Every cell in her body might shriek in protest at inviting him to sleep in her house, but she couldn't refuse without a damn good reason. "Your truck wouldn't start?"

He gave her a sheepish grin. "My shoulder's too sore to put on the chains."

The reminder of his injury stabbed her conscience. She stood rooted while he shrugged off his jacket. Despite his pain, he hadn't shirked from the task of protecting Nicholas. The least she could do was put him up for the night. Even if she'd never sleep a wink.

"Come on, then." She strived to keep her voice even. "The couch opens into a bed."

She avoided a direct look at the telling glimmer in Logan's eyes, almost as if he knew how uncomfortable having him here would be for her. Spinning on her heel, she headed toward the den, stopping only to tug linens and blankets from a hall closet. After helping him make up the bed, she left him on his own for the night.

TARA AWAKENED to the aroma of coffee and frying bacon. After tossing and turning most of the night, she'd finally fallen asleep in the early hours of the morning. Nicholas usually arose at the crack of dawn to demand breakfast, and a glance at the clock told her it was just past ten.

Nicholas!

At the sight of his empty crib, Tara's heart pummeled her ribs. Throwing off the covers, she shot out of bed, raced down the hall in her T-shirt and skidded into the kitchen.

Nicholas sat happily in his high chair, sharing breakfast with his dinosaur, smearing bits of scrambled egg and toast across his tray. Logan stood at the stove and removed crisp bacon from a frying pan while a stranger sat at the kitchen table. The morning sun glinted off a badge at his belt.

"Good morning, sleepyhead," Logan teased.

"Nicholas! How did... Who is... What are you...?" She closed her mouth, which didn't seem to be working properly. Tara plucked Nicholas from his chair, and with him secure in her arms, her panic subsided. Once again she'd made a fool of herself. Logan must have heard Nicholas and taken him from her room so she could sleep. A thoughtful gesture.

Still, the idea of Logan entering her room while she slept irritated her. She would have said so if the police detective wasn't already giving her the once-over, a guarded expression plastered across his freckled face.

Logan deftly broke an egg into the pan while making introductions. "Tara Larson, meet Detective Mike Scott, an old friend, Penny's brother, and a member of Harden's finest."

Recalling Penny's emergency, Tara did her best to remember her manners. "How's your grandmother?"

"Not good. She broke her leg when she fell, so I'm afraid Penny won't be available to baby-sit for a while."

"I understand." Tara nodded, uncomfortably aware of her bare feet and legs exposed below her long T-shirt. What must they think of her, racing into the kitchen half dressed, with a wild look in her eye? She hoped they couldn't see the heat flushing her face. "I'll change Nicholas and be back in a few minutes."

The detective took a sip of coffee, leaned back in his chair and crossed his ankle over a knee. "No hurry, ma'am."

"The omelet's almost ready," Logan called after her as she fled with as much dignity as she could.

Logan smiled and loaded the eggs with cheese, onion and green pepper filling. Although he experienced a twinge of guilt over the panic in Tara's eyes, he couldn't help noticing how good she looked with that tousled just-out-of-bed hair, sexy T-shirt without a bra, and those flawless, forever-long legs.

She returned a few minutes later, wearing baggy jeans and a bulky sweater that hid her sexy curves, and put Nicholas down in his playpen with several plastic trucks.

Logan had already set the table with the yellow place mats and neon pink napkins he'd found hidden at the bottom of the silverware drawer. Tara poured herself orange juice from the pitcher, spine stiff, lips set firm, as if steeling herself to answer some tough questions.

Mike set down his coffee cup and opened a notepad. "Logan filled me in on some background and told me what happened. Where were you when the kidnapper entered the premises?"

"Excuse me?" Coffee sloshed into the saucer, and she stared at Mike in amazement over the rim of her cup. If she was acting, she had to be one of the finest actresses Logan had ever seen. But he'd been fooled before—by the best of them.

Her tone rose in flabbergasted amazement. "Am I a suspect? Why would I steal my own son?"

Logan shook his head and raised his brows in his best I-told-you-so expression, which his old friend ignored. Although Mike had to do his job, he was walking up the wrong side of the street with that line of questioning.

Mike clicked the top of his pen, his hand poised over his notepad. "Stranger things have happened. I have to be thorough, consider every possibility, before I discount anyone. Are you involved in a custody battle with your ex?"

"Not unless he has a direct line from hell."

At her bitter words, Mike's head jerked up, and he gave Tara a hard stare, which she met with equanimity. Mike was the first to look away. For someone who appeared so vulnerable, why didn't Tara play the grieving widow? Logan couldn't figure her. But then he hadn't figured out Allison, either, until it was too late.

During the awkward pause, Logan limped around the packed boxes to the table and placed a fragrant omelet on her plate. "I forgot to tell you, Tara's a widow."

Mike's pen scrawled across the notepad, and Tara blotted her spilled coffee with a napkin. "Have there been any prior attempts to take the child?"

"No." She cut the omelet with the edge of her fork and moved the food around on her plate, but never raised the fork to her lips.

Mike shifted in his chair. "Can you think of anyone who would want to take your child?"

"Conrad Pemberton, my former father-in-law, has threatened to take Nicholas away from me." Only her fingers twisting the napkin in her lap betrayed her agitation. "But I stopped worrying about him after I consulted an attorney."

"Why?"

"The law is clear on this. A child cannot be taken from his mother unless the mother is unfit."

Logan was glad his old friend had been on duty this morning when he'd called the station. The questioning could get rough, but Mike would make this as easy as possible for Tara without compromising the investigation.

Mike leaned forward with a frown and a gleam in his warm brown eyes. "What better way to establish you're a bad mother than to prove you can't keep track of your child?"

Tara shook her head. "I don't think so. Conrad Pemberton has no idea where I am. Besides, he may be an old-fashioned male chauvinist who believes the only place a woman belongs is at home with her children, but he would never resort to anything illegal."

"Why?"

She hesitated as if weighing her words with care. "He's rich, a pillar of his community."

Logan frowned at her hesitation. What could she be hiding? What had she left out of her clipped explanation? He turned off the stove, took a seat beside Tara and resisted the urge to comfort her with a pat on the arm or a squeeze of her hand. After Allison, he hesitated to offer comfort to a woman who so obviously had secrets. Besides, it was likely Mike wanted her rattled, wanted her honest response without her considering every word with care.

Mike gave Logan a stern look, warning him not to interrupt, then turned back to Tara. "Did you and Pemberton get along while your husband was alive?"

Tara shrugged. "The old man tolerated me."

"How long ago did your husband die?"

"Less than a year." If Tara was making any attempt to hide her relief over her husband's demise, Logan couldn't spot it. What kind of woman was she? Would she marry a rich man's son for the money? Was that any different from using a man to advance a career, as Allison had done? Hell, none of this was his concern.

Mike pulled a business card out of his pocket and handed it to Tara. Logan thought his friend had finished with his questions, but it appeared he'd only used his card to distract her and make his question seem more casual. "The situation with Conrad Pemberton has recently worsened?"

She sighed, and stood to place the card in a drawer. "We don't speak."

"Why?"

"He believes his grandson can't be properly raised without a country club membership." Tara slammed the drawer shut and walked over to pick up Nicholas. "But I don't see how this is relevant. How do you know the attempt to take my son wasn't part of the kidnapping ring in the news?"

"That's possible," Mike admitted. "Just the same, we'll check Pemberton's whereabouts last night." He regarded her with a somber look. "Are you in any kind of trouble?"

Tara's voice sharpened. "What do you mean?"

"Do you owe money? Are you being blackmailed? Is there a jealous boyfriend in the woodwork?"

"No, no. Nothing like that."

Logan studied her reactions. She was hiding something. Then again, maybe her discomfort stemmed from the personal nature of the questions.

"Do you think I should leave Harden?" Tara asked.

Mike shook his head. "Chances are, with the back door left open, Nicholas was picked at random. And if that's the case, statistically, the chance of the kidnapper returning is infinitesimal."

"And if he wasn't picked at random?"

"It's unlikely. But whoever wants him can follow you. And you can't hide forever. Sooner or later you'd have to break cover. My advice is to be careful, but go on with your everyday activities."

Logan changed the topic slightly, hoping to erase the trapped and frustrated grimace from Tara's face. "Any leads on the kidnapping ring?"

Mike tapped the end of his pen against the pad. "I'm not free to discuss most of the details. One child was taken from his home, one from a grocery store, and another from a shopping center. I'm not going to jump to conclusions. Do you mind if I have a look around and dust for prints?"

"Please. Go ahead."

From his position on Tara's hip, Nicholas reached for a slice of bacon. "Eat."

At least someone appreciated his cooking. Tara hadn't swallowed a bite. The men pushed back their chairs, and Logan started to clear the table.

Tara broke off a tiny bit of bacon for Nicholas. "I'll get the dishes." She swung the baby to her other hip. "Detective, are you going to post an officer to protect my son?"

"I'm afraid we don't have the manpower for that. But as soon as the roads are plowed, I'll have a patrol car make more regular sweeps of the neighborhood. If you notice anyone skulking about, any strange cars cruising the streets, or receive any threatening calls, phone me."

"By tonight, every door will have a dead bolt," Logan told Mike. They walked to the back door, and Mike opened his crime scene kit and began brushing the door for prints.

"Do you need any help?" Logan asked.

As Tara placed cups into the dishwasher, Mike clapped Logan on the shoulder. "Yeah. You can entertain me while I work. Didn't I hear somewhere you did the stunt work on Stallone's new movie?"

Logan laughed. "I injured my knee on that film. The car rolled over four times before hurtling into the air and landing atop a barge in the Mississippi. The roll bar saved my life."

"And the knee?"

"That's the reason I'm back in Jersey."

The door closed behind the men, and Tara busied herself with the dishes. Logan reentered, went into the garage for a snow shovel and headed back out. The sounds of snow being scraped off the back steps echoed dully through the door.

An hour later, when Tara was halfway through reading *The Cat in the Hat* to Nicholas, the men joined her in the den. At their grim expressions, she clutched Nicholas tight. "Did you find any prints?"

Mike shook his head. "Nothing usable. Lots of smudges. But when Logan shoveled snow off the back landing, we found this." He held up a see-through plastic bag. Inside was a man's large leather glove.

Tara felt the blood drain from her face.

Logan took a step toward her, but Mike held him back by grabbing his arm. "Do you recognize it?"

"Can I have a better look?" She held out a shaking hand, her throat tight.

Even through the plastic, she could feel the quality of the butter-soft leather. Peeling back the inner wrist of the glove, she checked for a tag. Nothing. Nor were there signs of wear on the palms or fingertips. Heart pounding, she turned the glove on its side to examine the stitching, searching for the imperfections that would reveal whether the glove was hand-sewn. Sure enough, the stitches were uneven. A sudden wave of faintness sent the room swirling.

"Conrad Pemberton wears gloves like this."

She set Nicholas on the floor to crawl, then slumped in the couch, her shoulders sagging. Would she ever be free of the Pembertons and their influence? She hadn't expected him to follow her to Harden.

But then, she hadn't expected it to be so difficult to shake off the past and memories of Joe. Just yesterday at the real estate office, she'd spotted a man who tilted his head at the same angle as Joe did. And her heart had given a lurch. But she'd resisted the impulse to follow him. Damn. Just when she'd rid herself of the most harrowing recollections of her husband, his father took up where he'd left off. It wasn't fair. She sighed. When had life ever been fair?

Mike paced beside the fireplace, and his impatient question jolted her thoughts back to the present. "How can you be sure the gloves are his?"

Tara sighed and ignored her queasy stomach. "I can't be positive, but the gloves are custom-made in Trenton. The stitches are sewn by hand, and the leather is the finest quality."

"I take it they're expensive."

She nodded. "Very."

"Thanks." Mike shot Logan a significant look before turning back to her. "You've been helpful. I'll be in touch."

While Mike showed himself out, Nicholas amused himself with ducking under a blanket and peeking out at them. At least the attempted kidnapping hadn't seemed to faze him.

Logan took a seat beside her on the couch. "Hey. Are you okay?"

Her head throbbed. Her voice shook. "No one can take my son from me. Especially that overbearing, pompous old man."

Logan placed an arm around her stiff shoulders. "I've known Mike since we were kids. Once he's on a case, no one digs deeper than he does. If your father-in-law is after Nicholas, Mike will put him behind bars for a long time."

"Conrad Pemberton buys his way out of trouble. Bending the law to suit his needs isn't difficult when he lunches with judges and senators."

Logan's voice roughened with frustration and exasperation. "Why would your father-in-law want the baby?"

"Conrad is the most domineering man I know. I feared and despised him from the first time we met. Before Joe died, I worked in a small real estate office as a receptionist. Joe was a freelance journalist who wrote at home, so he took care of Nicholas. At the time, my father-in-law may have disapproved of my working, but that's the way Joe wanted it." And whatever Joe wanted, Joe got.

She took a deep breath to rid herself of the bitterness in her voice. "After Joe's death, Conrad made his views known. He insisted that I should stay home from work and raise my son. A day-care center or babysitter wasn't good enough for his grandson."

Logan's tone was nonjudgmental. "And you disagreed?"

"I had no choice. If we wanted to eat, I had to work."

"Didn't Joe have life insurance?"

"He didn't care enough about his family to protect us." She spoke calmly, glad that her voice didn't shake. "I was let go from my job because of Nicholas, and when I couldn't find work anywhere else, I realized how many strings Conrad could pull. I sold the house and furnishings and lived off the equity from the sale while I earned my real estate license. When Barbara offered me a place to stay, I thought my luck was finally turning, thought Harden would be the perfect town to escape Conrad's influence."

Logan frowned and raised a brow, obviously not buying her sketchy story. "How could he expect you to take care of Nicholas without an income?"

"Oh, he offered to support us."

Logan cocked his head to the side and waited.

"For a price." And it was a price Tara refused to pay. Never again would she forfeit her hard-won independence. She didn't expect Logan to understand. No man could. But she had no intention of explaining her reasons to him.

His arm around her shoulders, and his thigh pressed against her leg, seemed too intimate. She got up from the couch, went to the kitchen and heated a bottle for Nicholas. Although her son didn't need help, when she returned to the den and took a seat in a chair across from Logan, she cuddled Nicholas as if he were still a newborn infant, gently rocking him.

Nicholas stared back at her, sucking hard, wide blue eyes watchful. The movement of the chair reassured him, and after he finished the milk, his lids drifted shut.

During the time she fed her baby, Logan had remained silent. Now she looked up to find him watching her, and she fidgeted under his blatant interest.

She wished Barbara had told her more about her cousin. Where did he live? What kind of family did he have? He was the first man to pique her interest in so long, the thoughts made her distinctly uneasy, since she wanted him to both stay and go. It would be too easy to depend on him. He'd already done so much for them. What would he do if she asked for his help?

No. Depending on a man was dangerous, an open invitation for him to take charge. She'd learned that the hard way. It'd be best to send Logan home.

She took a deep breath. "I'll put him to bed and help you dig out the truck."

She carried the baby to his bedroom, tucked him into his crib and handed him his dinosaur. After smoothing his hair off his brow, she planted a light kiss on his cheek. So sweet. So vulnerable, with only her to protect him. She stepped to the doorway, then hesitated, turned back, checked the window lock and pulled the drapes closed.

FAILURE.

Puddles of melted snow dissipated on the hallway floor, evaporating just like the plan to snatch Nicholas. Even now the fear would not release its hold. An ominous stillness hung over the empty foyer, and the air quivered with a cloudy, unnatural haze, as warm breath fogged the mirror.

Being in Tara's house, touching her things, holding her son, had sliced open oozing wounds. Few who knew or saw Tara now would have guessed the truth. When had she grown so strong? She'd thrown away old pictures, taken back her maiden name. Started over.

And how dare she bring a man into her life and home? He didn't belong there, interfering, disrupting carefully laid plans.

Huge and menacing, the interfering fool had crept into the room with a stealth surprising for one so large. He'd remained silent, then pounced with surprising speed, ripping the baby away with the force of a tornado.

The violent exchange had caused aches and bruises, but such injuries could be overcome. But who was the man at Tara's house? *What was he doing there, keeping me from the baby?*

Baby. The word evoked visceral pain. A gloved fist yanked off a wig and battled the desire to smash the mirror. Bare fingers of the other hand were numb from the cold. Though the fireplace was blazing, its warmth didn't penetrate the frozen knot of revenge inside.

Damn the man! New plans would have to be made.

WHEN TARA STEPPED OUTSIDE, the sun hid behind a haze of clouds, but still, she squinted at the brightness reflecting off the snow. Asleep in his crib with the monitor next to him, Nicholas would be fine. She was only going out in the front yard for a few minutes to help Logan scoop out a path to the street.

As she made her way down the already-cleared sidewalk with the baby monitor in hand, her boots crunched on tiny particles of ice. The plows had cleared the road, but piles of snow blocked the drive and prevented Logan's departure. "How's the shoulder?"

"Sore. I'm not lifting much weight at one time."

"You shouldn't be digging at all."

"I need to get to a hardware store. I'll feel better when you have dead bolts on every door."

When she came alongside him, he stopped digging, planted the shovel in the snow and leaned against the handle. He hadn't shaved, and the dark stubble emphasized his sturdy jaw and razor-sharp cheekbones. As usual, his dark eyes held and tried to capture hers, testing her resolve.

"You're sure you and Nicholas want to stay here alone tonight?"

That was as close as he had come to offering to stay, and she appreciated the easy way he had of leaving the decision up to her. He didn't press, yet he made his thoughts clear, all without saying one word denigrating her ability to decide for herself.

Tara propped the baby monitor on the truck. "We'll be fine. I can't spend the rest of my life running or hiding." Unwilling to face his searching stare, she reached for the shovel. He straightened and rubbed his shoulder, tacitly turning over the chore without protest. She dug the blade into the snow behind the rear tire of his truck. "Rest for a few minutes and tell me why the kidnapper went out the back door."

"What do you mean?"

"Well, you were in the bedroom. The front door would've been a closer exit."

For the first time since she'd moved in, the house's isolation in a subdivision seemed less appealing than a more crowded apartment building. Barbara's two-acre lot backed up to several others. Anyone could slip across the woods in back and follow the small creek out of the subdivision, and the canvas windscreen on the neighbor's tennis court provided a good cover for hiding.

Logan shrugged as if testing his shoulder and considering taking back the shovel. "Perhaps the getaway car was hidden one street over. It's a shame the snow covered the tracks you saw leading into the woods."

And it was a shame Logan hadn't gotten a glimpse of his assailant. But she didn't say it aloud. If she was going to set about wishing, she'd wish the whole incident had never happened.

Stopping for a moment, she leaned the shovel against the truck. "I'll be right back, I just want to check Nicholas."

Nicholas slept soundly, and when she stepped outside again, the sun shone brightly. Across the street, several neighborhood kids had come out and were building a snowman, and a dog leaped and yapped, getting in their way.

Grinning, she searched for Logan. He was kneeling on the far side of the truck, adjusting chains around the tire. She reached for the shovel.

Thrusting the shovel deep with her boot, she lifted the snow and dumped it to the side of the drive. Her breath came out in white puffs. She kept waiting for

Logan to ask for the shovel, and when he didn't, she assumed his shoulder was worse than he let on.

The first snowball pinged on the shovel's handle. The second landed on her head with a plop and rained soft snow over her face, in her collar, down her back.

Squealing at Logan's playfulness, she dropped the shovel and dived for cover behind his truck. Perfect for snowballs, the newly fallen snow packed into lightweight ammunition. She gathered several scoops, and when his face popped over the hood, she lobbed three fast ones in his direction.

"Missed me," he teased, catching a snowball and throwing it back.

She grinned. "Liar." One of her snowballs had made contact, and she'd seen his eyes widen when it harmlessly hit his chest. She stooped for more snow, intent on soaking him.

An arm came from behind and toppled her to the soft snow.

"Logan, you rat. What about your shoulder?"

His eyes crinkled at the corners. "I landed on my good side."

"You have a good side?"

"It's about time you smiled."

They rolled together, he ending up on his stomach with her across his back. She scrambled for leverage, scooped some snow in her mitten and slipped it under his scarf.

"That's cheating." He roared with mock outrage at the same time turning beneath her until she sat on his stomach. "I should wash your face in snow."

She chuckled. "I'm already cold enough. Thank you." The urge to plant a kiss on his laughing lips nearly overwhelmed her. She leaned forward, his mouth inches from hers, drawing her like a seductive sorcerer.

Suddenly she realized her position astride him. Maybe Logan really was different from Joe, she thought with a reckless optimism. And maybe the moon was made of cottage cheese.

Clearing her throat to fill the suddenly awkward moment, she suppressed a shudder and tensed with feelings of regret. How had she let him get so close?

"I should check Nicholas again."

Almost as if he'd expected her reaction, he let her go without a word of protest. Did he think she was playing games, leading him on, then backing away? She fled to the house, ashamed of herself for responding to an attraction she wouldn't pursue, unsure when the playful moment had turned significant and serious.

Hastening through the front door, she threw her scarf and mittens onto a bench. Once she held Nicholas, the child would help erase the confusion still buffeting through her like snowflakes on a midwinter's day.

Unzipping her parka, she strode to the bedroom. With every footstep taking her farther from Logan, her confidence grew. She could take care of Nicholas by herself. She'd done fine during the last ten months.

Logan might mean well, but she had no interest in repeating the mistakes of her past. Joe Pemberton had also been the most charming of men—until the day she married him. She flushed and remembered her naïveté, the hope that if she tried hard enough, changed enough, Joe would love her. But he never had, and she'd never known why. She often wondered why he'd married her in the first place. However, now that her husband was gone, she wouldn't play the hypocrite and pretend to mourn a death that had set her free and given her back her son.

Lost in thought, she reached Nicholas's room. The door stood ajar and a triangle of light beamed into the hallway. Her brow wrinkled. Hadn't she shut the door? And why wasn't Nicholas demanding her attention?

She heard his giggle and smiled, ready to greet him and whirl him around in her arms. She pushed the door open slowly without making a sound and sought his little face beaming at her from behind the bars of the crib.

But instead of the baby's grinning face, she confronted the back of a stranger standing over his crib.

Chapter Five

"Get away from him!"

Tara lunged toward Nicholas, her heart beating faster than a hummingbird's wings. The stranger had no business in her house, in her child's room, With arms outstretched to snatch her son from possible harm, she elbowed the chestnut-haired woman away from the crib. When Tara seized Nicholas, he screamed and round tears ran down his chubby cheeks.

The stranger backed away, her high-pitched, singsong tone contrite. "Sorry."

Tara twisted around, her jacket whipping the bars of the crib. Cuddling Nicholas close, she glared at the stranger. "What are you doing in my house? How did you get in? I'm calling the police."

The woman rolled her eyes. "Hey, take it easy."

Take it easy? Was the woman nuts? Wide-eyed, Nicholas clung to her as she observed the other woman. When her own features stared back from the other's face, a wave of dizziness hit her. Then the stranger stepped into the window's light, and the uncanny resemblance lessened. The brunette, about two inches taller than Tara, wore an expensive but dated red leather jacket and black pants that tucked neatly into scuffed leather boots. A silk scarf around her forehead gave her a campy look.

"Yoo-hoo! Anyone home?" Another female voice echoed down the hall.

Tara's heart cramped, and she clutched Nicholas tighter. Perspiration beaded under her arms. Her thoughts whirled in confusion. Who were these women and why were they here? Were they after Nicholas? Please, let Logan limp through the door. She started to take a step toward the hall, but the stranger in the bedroom held her empty hands palm up and shot Tara a hesitant smile. "Sorry I startled you."

Nicholas hiccuped. Tara's voice quivered. "What are you doing here?"

"I'm Marge Henley, your back-door neighbor." Marge gestured toward the rear of the house, then held out her hand for Tara to shake. When Tara didn't respond, the woman dropped her hand to her side and her grin faded. "I came over with a casserole to welcome you to the neighborhood but no one answered my knock. I was going to leave, but I heard the baby crying."

"Crying?" Tara's gaze flew to the baby monitor. Why hadn't *she* heard Nicholas?

"I stuck my head in the door and called out. When no one answered and the baby kept crying, I put the casserole I brought you on the counter and checked to make sure nothing was wrong." She smiled tentatively. "I suppose this does seem strange, but around here we try and look out for one another. We even have a crime watch."

Tara recalled her earlier senseless fear when she wakened to find Nicholas gone, only to find Logan feeding him breakfast. The memory settled her. She couldn't return to that state of constant apprehension when she'd imagined Joe's ghost stalking around every corner. That was behind her now. But despite her determination, putting her suspicions aside proved difficult, especially after last night.

She grabbed the baby monitor in her free hand. "How'd you get in?"

Marge shrugged. "The back door was open."

Had Mike and Logan left the door unlocked? In the confusion of the morning, Tara couldn't remember. Jiggling Nicholas in her arms, she patted his back to quiet his hiccups. "Sorry. I'm edgy. Someone broke into my house yesterday."

Sudden understanding smoothed out the slight wrinkle on Marge's brow. "Did they take anything? Did they catch the burglar?"

Before Tara could answer, the other woman, who had called out a moment ago, stepped into the room. In this subdivision, people seemed to just walk into other people's houses without an invitation. Tall and broad-shouldered, she sauntered in with a friendly smile and a toss of her curly auburn mane. "I thought I heard you, Marge. Hi, I'm Ruthie Raines."

"Umm. I'm Tara Larson, and this is my son, Nicholas."

Ruthie's warm green eyes targeted on the baby. "Oh, what a darling child. Hello, Nicholas. Will you come to Miss Ruthie?" She held out her arms to the baby, but Tara pulled back.

Marge chuckled, leaned forward and chucked Nicholas under the chin. "Don't mind Ruthie, she wouldn't hurt a flea. She's a baby nut. If she had her way, she'd give the old woman in the shoe competition."

Ruthie sighed, picked up Nicholas's dinosaur from the floor where he'd dropped it, and handed it to him. "I'd love to have kids, but we've just about given up hope. You don't know what I'd do for an adorable little guy like him."

The women spoke in normal tones, and Nicholas's cries and hiccups diminished, but Tara's heart still thudded against her ribs. Get a grip. Forcibly relaxing the tense set of her shoulders, she eased her grasp on Nicholas. Just because Ruthie couldn't have children of her own didn't mean she was out to kidnap Nicholas, and Marge might be a busybody, but her intentions seemed sincere.

Still, she had no intention of handing Nicholas over to Ruthie, who was so obviously eager to hold him. Not until she checked out their stories. "Why don't we go into the kitchen, and I'll fix his snack?"

The last of Nicholas's tears disappeared. "Eat. Eat."

During the walk down the hall, Tara checked the monitor and decided the batteries must be dead. Despite her efforts to believe in these women, she remained uneasy. But when she reached the kitchen and spied Marge's casserole dish on the counter, the remainder of her suspicions dispersed like clouds on a windy day. "Would either of you like coffee or hot chocolate?"

Marge smiled. "Coffee would be great."

"And it'll give us a chance to get to know this cute little guy," Ruthie agreed.

Her neighbors took seats at the breakfast bar while Tara put Nicholas in his high chair. Opening the kitchen cabinet, she took out jars of baby food for Nicholas and put on a pot of coffee.

"So who's the handsome hunk outside with the shovel?" Marge asked.

"Logan Stone," Tara answered. "He's doing some carpentry work for me."

Marge's gaze wandered to the mattress on the floor of the adjoining den. "Have you known him long?"

Tara's face burned at the woman's implication.

Before she could answer, Ruthie saved her. "Logan grew up in the neighborhood. He and Mike Scott are old friends."

Nicholas pointed at cookies Tara laid out on the counter for her neighbors. "Eat."

Tara shook her head. "First, you need some good food inside you." She peeled a banana and handed pieces of it to Nicholas.

Marge drummed her long nails on the Formica countertop. "So they've been friends since..."

"High school," Ruthie replied with an amused grin. "I run into Logan's sisters in the grocery store occasionally. For a while, Eve was real worried about her brother."

Tara raised her brow. "Oh? Do you know Logan?"

"Not personally. He and Mike were behind me in school. I shouldn't gossip," Ruthie muttered, though it was clear she was dying to impart some juicy story.

Marge leaned forward. "I can keep a secret."

"It's no secret. In Hollywood, some woman pretended to fall in love with him, but she was just using him."

Marge's mouth firmed into a petulant pout. "Logan probably told his sister that to win her sympathy." Her eyes shot Tara a catty glance. "With his looks, he likely has dozens of women."

Ruthie shook her head. "I don't think so. Eve told me this woman broke his heart."

"So Logan will be returning to Hollywood as soon as his heart heals," Marge guessed.

Was that why Tara felt so drawn to Logan? Deep down, he was hurting just like she was.

"His sister thought he might stay." Ruthie made herself at home in the kitchen and poured fresh coffee.

Determined not to let the fact that Logan might leave town affect her, Tara remained silent and coaxed some mashed peas into Nicholas's mouth.

"Come on. What man would remain in Harden when he could live in Hollywood and work with the stars?" Marge asked.

Obviously enjoying the gossip about Logan, Ruthie waved her hands wide and chuckled while glancing at Tara in open speculation. "Maybe the right woman might change his mind."

At Ruthie's more-than-casual perusal, Tara made a lame attempt at a disinterested smile. The air in the kitchen suddenly seemed close and still.

Odd how Tara now knew more about Logan's past than Joe's. Her former husband would never speak about the times before they met, but occasionally at parties she'd heard rumors about an old love affair he'd had with a girl named Janice Wilson that had ended abruptly. No one had ever shared the details with her, and she'd learned not to ask about her.

Although twinges of guilt stabbed her conscience and she knew she should change the subject, Tara couldn't resist listening to her neighbors' conversation. Despite her attempt to maintain her distance, Ruthie had piqued her curiosity about Logan.

Marge leaned forward, her eyes glittering. "Is he seeing anyone in Harden?"

Ruthie stared out the window for a long moment. Finally she answered. "No. I thought... I was wondering why Logan's here."

"For protection." Ruthie twirled her cup and narrowed her eyes. "I heard someone tried to kidnap Tara's son."

"Kidnap?" Marge gasped.

Tara's gaze slid to Ruthie and held the other woman's stare. "How did you know that?"

Ruthie reached over and patted Tara's shoulder. "Penny's grandmother broke her leg last night. I called to see how she was doing. Mike had filled his sister in, and Penny told me what happened." Ruthie shrugged.

"That's why I moved to Harden." Marge took a sip of coffee and grimaced. "Everyone here looks out for their neighbors."

Thankful she wouldn't have to relate the terrifying details, Tara wiped mashed banana from Nicholas's face and set him down. "Have either of you noticed strangers hanging around the neighborhood?"

Marge blotted her lips with a napkin and shoved the coffee away. "Nope. Mike asked me this morning, though at the time I had no idea why he was asking."

"I can't remember anything odd around here. No one new has moved in lately, except you and Marge." Ruthie's eyes flicked to the casserole on the counter. "I see she brought you one of her scrumptious turkey casseroles."

Tara turned to Marge. "And I never thanked you. Nicholas and I will have it for dinner."

As Ruthie watched Nicholas stack Tupperware containers on the floor, a wistful look came over her face. She sighed. "You're so lucky to have such an adorable little boy. I'd do just about anything to have one like him." She took a quick sip of coffee and chuckled. "Come to think of it, I have done just about everything."

"She's had all those fertility tests done, but the doctors couldn't find anything wrong," Marge added softly.

Nicholas toddled over to their visitors, and Ruthie lifted him into her lap, where he played with her amber necklace. "The doctors told Hal and me to keep trying." She snorted. "Doctors! What do they know? By the time we gave up hope, the adoption agency turned us down. They said we were too old."

Marge drummed her nails on the countertop as if she had more on her mind than her simple words. "It's a shame. Ruthie would make a great mother."

The redhead edged her coffee cup away from Nicholas's grasping fingers. "Maybe I could watch Nicholas for you until Mrs. Scott's better and Penny can take over."

The thought of again leaving Nicholas with anyone made Tara break out into a cold sweat. Penny, so protective of Nicholas and careful to keep him safe, would have been the perfect sitter. And she'd come with Barbara's recommendation. But leaving him with a stranger?

The front door banged, saving her from having to reply to Ruthie's offer, and Logan's uneven steps thumped down the hall. "My truck's free," he called out, his deep voice cheerful. "Just thought I'd check the door to the garage before I buy the hardware."

He limped into the kitchen, and when he spotted Tara's company, his brows rose.

"Marge Henley and Ruthie..." Tara began.

"Raines," the other woman supplied.

"... Are my neighbors. This is Logan Stone." Tara made the introductions and watched the women's reactions to Logan's rugged appearance. He seemed to take up more than his share of the kitchen, and Ruthie's gaze kept darting in his direction.

Marge leaned against the counter, assessing Logan in a long stare. Her voice purred. "So, you're the handyman."

"Tara hired me to babyproof the house."

Tara stared in disbelief. Was Marge coming on to him, or had Tara's fear thrown her whole perspective out of whack?

When Ruthie looked from Logan to Marge and shook her head, Tara suspected her suspicion might be right on target. With an apologetic glance at Tara, Ruthie set Nicholas back down. "Well, I should go. Thanks for the coffee. If you ever need a sitter, call me. I'd love to take Nicholas off your hands for a while."

She rumpled Nicholas's hair and waved goodbye. Tara walked to the front door with her. Nicholas followed, and Tara scooped him up. "Bye-bye."

When Tara returned to the kitchen, Marge patted her flat stomach with a confidential smile. "I didn't want to make a big deal in front of Ruthie since she is having trouble getting pregnant, but I'm expecting a baby soon."

Logan's mouth twisted wryly as if he were uninterested in woman's talk. "Excuse me. I have work to do." Taking a tape from his pocket, he measured the thickness of the door leading to the garage for the new dead bolt. After meticulously noting the dimensions on a small pad, he stuffed the results into the front pocket of his shirt. Disregarding Marge, he squatted down and checked the door's hinge.

"Congratulations," Tara said to make up for Logan's disinterest.

"Down!" From her arms, Nicholas pointed toward the floor.

Tara set him down by her feet where she could keep watch on him. "When's your baby due?"

Either Marge didn't hear, or she ignored Tara's question. With a swish of her hips and a gleam in her eyes, she leaned over Logan. "I might need your services at my house."

Her seductive tone left a lingering doubt in Tara's mind about what kind of services Marge had in mind. Just what kind of woman—particularly a pregnant one—would put the make on a stranger? Immediately, Tara felt guilty. In her own emotional state, she could be reading Marge wrong. And who was she to judge, anyway?

While she didn't expect Logan to redden in embarrassment at her neighbor's forwardness, she was surprised to see his eyes turn cold as river ice.

"What kind of services did you have in mind, Mrs....?"

"Henley. But *you* can call me Marge." The woman licked her bottom lip. "With the baby kidnapping ring snatching children right out of their homes, I thought you could come over and make my place safe."

"But you don't even have a baby yet," Tara said.

Marge fluttered her hand in the air. "I've waited a long time, and I want everything perfect before my baby arrives."

Logan reached into his back pocket, opened his wallet and pulled out a business card. "I don't usually do this kind of work but—"

"I'd be willing to pay whatever you ask."

She took a moment too long to take the card from Logan's fingers. For lack of something to do, Tara cleared the counter of coffee cups and wiped it clean.

Marge slipped Logan's card into her pocket, and Tara urged her toward the door. "I still have a lot of unpacking to do. Thanks again for the casserole."

"Enjoy it."

When she was finally gone, Tara let out a sigh of relief. Her neighbors seemed affable enough, but they'd given her quite a scare. Briefly she wondered if the hormones from Marge's pregnancy were making her act like a third-rate hooker, or was she that way all the time?

The wind, which held the whistle of a pending crisis, subsided for an instant, leaving utter silence in the kitchen. As Logan stared at Nicholas, his lips cracked into a grin. The sun peeked briefly through the threatening storm clouds, spilling golden rays onto Nicholas's blond hair and creating a halo around his face.

Nicholas had used the cabinet handle to pull himself to his feet. He balanced against the cabinet with one hand, and took several steps. Then he let go and stood without holding on. He moved one foot forward.

Tara held her breath and whispered, "He's walking."

She yearned to run for the camera to capture his first effort, but she didn't want to miss one second of this momentous occasion. His first steps. Her son was walking.

With a silly, yet endearing, grin still plastered across his face, Logan knelt on the tile and held out his arms to Nicholas. "You can do it, pal. Come on. Come to me."

With five rapid steps, the child tottered into Logan's arms. "Good boy." Logan praised the beaming boy.

Nicholas laughed, his cheeks rosy, and mimicked Logan's words. "Good boy."

Logan's large hands spanned Nicholas's waist, and he turned him to face Tara. "Now walk to your mama."

"Mama. Mama. Mama." He chanted her name with every step and waved his chubby arms for balance. He teetered, almost fell, then took two more steps. His face lit with proud excitement, his wide smile showing off his four front teeth, as if he knew he'd done something special and magical.

As she clasped her arms tightly around him, Tara swallowed a lump in her throat and kissed the baby-soft skin of his neck. For a moment she couldn't speak. Inhaling the scent of cornstarch powder and baby oil, she realized once more how close she'd come to losing this precious child. If Logan hadn't kept him safe yesterday, she would never have seen his first steps.

She glanced up at Logan, unashamed of the tears brimming from her eyes. Joe would have mocked her happiness, but Logan just grinned wider. Taking a folded handkerchief from his back pocket, he scooted closer and gently dabbed the moistness from her cheeks.

"Thanks. I guess I'm being silly," she said, sniffing. Joe would have called her overly emotional, irrational and stupid. Logan put his arm around her shoulder, and they sat on the floor while Nicholas crawled to play with his toys, already forgetting his newest accomplishment.

Logan couldn't have enjoyed himself more if Nicholas had been his son. Reveling in the homey kitchen, warmed by Tara's excitement over her son's achievement, he didn't want to leave. The instant that thought hit him, he took his arm from her shoulders and rose.

"I'd better see about those locks." He hurried out the front door to his truck before he did something really stupid—like kiss Tara. One more minute and he would have forgotten skinny blondes weren't his type.

He backed the truck down the driveway, his fingers clenched around the wheel. He couldn't give in to his feelings for Tara. She wasn't the kind of woman he could get out of his blood after one night, a week or even several months.

"All women aren't like Allison," his sister Eve had protested when she had tried to set him up on a blind date with one of her friends.

"It's none of your business," he'd pointed out, knowing she meant well but unwilling to discuss his feelings. And now he resented Tara for making him care.

When it came to women, he didn't trust his judgment, and rather than set himself up for a nasty fall, he'd be better off giving Tara a refund to hire someone else for the job.

The thought made his heart contract. Someone else might not drive through the snow. Someone else might not install the locks today. And if anything bad happened, Logan would never forgive himself.

Swerving his truck around a snowbank, he fought for emotional control. The double whammy of guarding the kid and consoling the mother brought out protective feelings he should ignore. He'd just stop at the hardware store, return and install the dead bolts, then forget Tara and her son.

The chances of the kidnapper returning were minuscule, and he couldn't spend every moment guarding against the possibility of another attempt. Mike would step up the patrols. Besides, Tara was right. They had to get on with their lives.

But how could he? Last night, he'd intended to work on an important bid—the subdivision blue-

prints that could mean the difference between winning a lucrative contract or going without work next
summer. The packet still waited on his desk, ready for
his precise calculations, and he still had time to pre-
pare the bid if he got right on it.

Ahead, the traffic light at the intersection was out
from the storm. Logan stopped, looked both ways,
and eased along the empty street. Although the plows
had cleared most of the roads, the schools were closed
while people braced for another storm.

He listened to the weather forecaster recommend
that everyone stay inside and off the roads. Suddenly,
the local news broke in with an announcement that
another child had been kidnapped in Harden. Except
for the child's description, no other details were given.

In the kitchen, Tara froze, then clicked off the station. She used a spatula to slide the last of the chocolate chip cookies from a baking pan to a plate, her
hands shaking.

The big sunny kitchen suddenly seemed too small.
She and Nicholas could use some fresh air, and they
couldn't spend the rest of their lives hiding from in-
visible threats.

"Come on, sweetheart. We're going for a walk."

"Eat?" Her son's blue gaze searched her face
hopefully.

"You can have one cookie later."

"Okay."

Another new word. Tara grinned while she bun-
dled him up, putting on his parka, boots and mittens,
before grabbing her own coat and stepping outside,
locking the door behind her. She turned and surveyed
the area for signs of lurking danger. Snow clung to the

branches of the fir trees, the additional weight bowing the needles. Sunshine glinted through icicles
hanging from the eaves and cast tiny rainbows onto
the windowpanes. Squirrels chirped and scampered
along the roof. Farther down the street, someone had
built a snowman with gravel eyes, a carrot nose and a
floppy fedora on its head. In the yard, children sled-
ded down a small incline, shrieking in delight. Most of
the neighbors had shoveled their driveways, and only
one car, a green Oldsmobile, drove slowly down the
street.

Was going outside foolhardy? Perhaps. While she
wanted to keep her son close to protect him, she
couldn't keep him away from people forever. They
couldn't spend the rest of their lives in hiding. A walk
and exercise would do them good.

After several turns around the block, she walked
back to the house and Nicholas rode on her shoulders. Her head was down to gauge her steps in the
snow. For an hour in the snow-washed air, she'd forgotten her troubles, but now they came back. Penny
would have to be replaced—and soon—or Tara would
lose her job. Should she put Nicholas in a day-care
center? Expose him to the inevitable colds and germs
inherent in places where so many children congregated? Or should she take Ruthie up on her offer?

Unhappy with either alternative and lost in thought,
she trudged past Logan's truck in the drive and retrieved her key from her pocket to unlock her front
door. She inserted the key in the lock and twisted, but
the key failed to turn. Perhaps she'd chosen the wrong
key. Before she could remove the key to examine it, the
door opened from the inside.

Logan loomed over her, his mouth twisted in a wry grin, and her breath caught at the spark of concern she imagined gleaming in his eyes. He held out a new key between thumb and forefinger. "I rekeyed the locks— just in case."

Nicholas grabbed for the shiny key, but Logan refused to let him have it. Instead, he reached into his pocket and pulled out a large red rubber ball.

The baby chuckled and took the ball with both hands, the key forgotten.

Tara's heart pounded. Why must Logan be so damned attractive? And considerate? She smothered her reaction to him with exasperation. "You rekeyed just in case... what? Do you think Barbara gave the kidnapper a key to the house?"

"Maybe she did," he replied with a husky catch. "She had housekeepers, carpet-cleaning people and contractors in and out all the time. We don't know who might have a key."

At his logical response, guilt stabbed her. Instead of making sarcastic comments, she should be thanking him. Yet the words of appreciation stuck in her throat. She couldn't help resenting the way she responded to him, instinctively leaning toward him and breathing in the leather scent of his jacket and the faint aroma of after-shave.

But her attraction didn't blind her to the fact he had made the decision for her, hadn't even discussed rekeying the locks. Like Joe. And Joe had always said he did it for her own good.

"Thank you." She finally got the words out.

Logan gave her a piercing look, but didn't comment. "Every door has a dead bolt, and this key unlocks them all. I also finished the rest of the job." He hesitated. "So I guess this is goodbye."

Nicholas waved the ball in his chubby hands. "Bye-bye."

Goodbye. Insecurities squashed the breath from her lungs. Joe was always threatening her with goodbyes. She'd been doing so well, and then with one little word, the old fears had snuck back, trapping her in the time before she'd learned the meaning of independence. How many times had Joe intimidated her?

Stop it. You don't need a man to tell you what to do. No matter how appealing she found Logan's help, she could get through this alone. For Nicholas's sake she had to be strong.

Her fingers clenched the new key. She commanded her feet to take one step, then another, into the foyer. Logan had already been around too long, and she had been reverting to form, depending on him instead of her own resourcefulness. He could become a habit, so she should feel relief at his departure, not regret.

She spoke softly. "Thank you for all you've done."

He hesitated, just an instant, before he ruffled Nicholas's hair playfully and gave her a warm smile. "If you need me, call."

She wouldn't. Couldn't. He turned and limped out of her life and into the dark. When he reached the driveway, she locked the door behind him and breathed deeply to relieve the heaviness in her chest.

"Eat." Nicholas tugged on her hair, and his action drew her thoughts to the task of feeding her son. Glad she'd bought enough groceries for a week and wouldn't have to drive through the snow, she headed for the kitchen.

She set Marge's turkey casserole in the microwave and turned it on. It was nearly heated when the phone rang. It was Mr. Bittner from the real estate office. He might have a client flying into town within the next day or so. Could she show a house despite the storm?

After reassuring him that she would be happy to help, she hung up the phone and had settled Nicholas into his high chair with a plastic duck, when the phone rang again.

"I want to see Nicholas," the all-too-familiar voice of her father-in-law, Conrad Pemberton, demanded over the line.

Her hand shook, and her first instinct was to hang up, but he would only call back. "How did you find me?"

"That doesn't matter. Do you realize you're denying me my rights and Nicholas his heritage?"

Fear coiled in her belly. "What do you mean?"

"I could go to court and sue for the right to see my grandson."

Rage shoved aside the fear. "You don't want to *see* him, you want to *own* him."

"He'd be better off with me. He'd have the best possible care, the best schools, a huge trust fund waiting for him. What could you possibly offer him that's better?"

Blind panic nearly overwhelmed her. "How about love?"

There was a silence before Conrad spoke. "Love?" He broke into a mocking laugh. "Will love feed him and clothe him? Will love pay for the doctors if he gets sick?"

Tara twisted the phone cord around her finger. "We'll get by."

"Getting by isn't good enough for my grandson!"

The old argument never changed. Sometimes the fear receded, allowing her a merciful ray of relief, but now, despite the bright kitchen lights, the icy dread hovered like a shadow over her.

"Stay away from us." Tara slammed the receiver down into the cradle. Running to Nicholas, she snatched him from the high chair to her breast. She'd *never* give him up. Never.

With her palm, she smoothed her son's head. His tiny chest rose and fell, and his foot kicked out. So precious. So vulnerable, with only her to protect him from the harsh world. She would do anything to keep him safe, to watch him grow, to see to it that he was nothing like his father.

She wouldn't let her father-in-law make her crazy. Nor would she let her father-in-law make her son into another cold, ruthless Pemberton. For her son, she wanted the best. She hoped he would turn out more like Logan Stone—kind, strong and caring.

She set Nicholas back in his chair, taking comfort in the ordinary movements of wiping off crumbs, unloading the dishwasher, pouring a glass of milk. She'd almost convinced herself Pemberton couldn't get to her here.

And then the lights went out.

Chapter Six

"Ma-ma?"

Fear, sharp and biting, stabbed Tara and drew her taut. The microwave ceased humming. In the darkness of the eerily silent kitchen, she groped for Nicholas, her breath stuck in her throat. Her hip knocked against the handle of a cabinet, shooting a pain down her side and a tremor through her body.

"Nicholas?"

Ah, there he was. She wrapped her hands around his waist and clung to him. What now? Why had the lights gone out?

With her son in her arms, she edged to the window without a sound. Pulling back the curtain, she peered through the oaks and across the backyard and spied dim lights through the fast-falling snow. Could her neighbor's house be in a different electric zone? Dropping the curtain into place, she hurried to the east window and saw more lights. Her pulse skittered. No one else had lost power. How was that possible? Had someone cut the power into her house? Was that someone after Nicholas?

The whistling wind sent icy drafts through the walls, and she shivered. The interior temperature already seemed to be dropping, and though the furnace used gas, it required electricity to work. The panel box was in the garage, but dare she go out to check? Why not? The garage door had a sturdy lock, and she wouldn't actually be leaving the house.

But someone could be waiting out there. Kidnappers? Her father-in-law? Joe's mocking laughter echoed in her mind, and she swallowed hard, banishing the bad memories. *Think. Don't let your imagination get the best of you.*

She drew a deep, steadying breath. Maybe she needed only to throw the breaker. Nicholas's hands were still warm, and she'd be in the cold garage only for a moment.

Tree branches scraped the windows, hurrying her through the hallway. She found a flashlight in the closet, then carried Nicholas through the den and into the chilly garage. Opening the breaker box, she shined the light inside but spotted nothing wrong.

Reentering the kitchen, she locked the door and checked the phone. Relief washed through her at the drone of the dial tone. Should she call the power company? No. She needed police protection. Balancing her yawning baby on her hip, she began to punch 911, then set the receiver down. She'd rather call Detective Mike Scott than a stranger who would waste time demanding long explanations.

Shining the flashlight into the drawer, she searched for his card, then dialed with trembling fingers. She waited with breath held. Would he be on duty? A bolt of relief went through her—at last, she heard his voice.

"Scott here."

Quickly she explained the situation over the background clicks of typing and shuffling papers and tried to keep the worry from her tone. "Can you come out right away?"

Through the phone a siren wailed, a woman shouted, a door clanged shut. Detective Scott swore under his breath. "It's probably nothing, but we need to be careful. Stay put and call the power company. I'll send someone out as soon as I can."

"Thanks." She redialed, reached a recording at the power company, and left a message.

Her heart beat wildly. Would Mike arrive within minutes or hours? She knew he'd do his best to come quickly, tried to convince herself he'd arrive before anyone broke into the house or she and Nicholas froze.

Another peek out the window revealed snow coming down harder than ever. It flurried thick and fast, covering the sidewalks and forming low drifts that blocked the road. Between the blizzard and the sounds of chaos she'd heard over the phone during her short call to Mike, she suspected it could be a while before he arrived.

Nicholas shivered, and Tara switched off the flashlight. She wouldn't give anyone outside a clue to her exact location. After retracing her steps to the bedroom in the dark by running one hand along the wall, she searched for Nicholas's snowsuit.

"It's okay, Nicholas. Mama's here with you."

Fumbling in the dark with his mittens, she listened for sounds that didn't belong. In the distance, a dog barked. A windowpane rattled, and she hoped it was caused by the rage of the wind storming the house.

"Eat."

She'd forgotten his supper. Her stomach churned. Only Nicholas could be hungry at a time like this. "Let's see what Mama can find."

She donned her jacket, and they returned to the kitchen. The turkey casserole in the microwave hadn't heated, so she popped it back into the refrigerator, then dug around in the cabinets and found a box of cereal. Perfect. Feeding Nicholas piece by piece should keep him quiet and occupied while they waited for help to arrive.

It seemed unlikely that the outage was unintentional. Could it only be a coincidence that someone had tried to kidnap her son, and that theirs was the sole house in the neighborhood that had lost power?

In the meantime, how could she defend them if necessary? Should she grab a knife? She had no knowledge of fighting, and if anyone broke in, they could easily disarm her. Besides, Nicholas could get hurt in a struggle. Thank God for Logan and the dead bolts. As long as they stayed inside, they'd be safe.

A half hour later, a vehicle slowly made its way down the road, the headlights streaking along the entry wall and turning into her drive. The engine purred, then shut off.

Heart frozen, she inched her way to the foyer and looked out the peephole, praying Nicholas would remain silent. A huge silhouette blocked the streetlight, and her mouth went dry. Detective Scott? He lifted his arm and thumped the door so loudly, she jumped back and dropped the cereal box.

"It's Logan Stone. Are you all right?"

At the familiar voice, Nicholas clapped and laughed. Tara exhaled a sigh of relief and unlocked the door. It might be normal to feel safer with a man around, but she couldn't remember having such feelings about Joe. Although torn between relief at Logan's friendly face and reluctance to spend more time with him, she had no choice but to let him in. Nicholas's safety might be at stake.

"Come in."

He strode through the doorway, then shut it firmly behind him. In the darkness she could feel him peering at her. "You okay?"

His husky voice warmed her like a sip of hot chocolate and eased the tense knot of worry in her chest.

"Yes. How'd you know—"

"Mike had an emergency and couldn't get away, so he called and asked me to check on you. Do you have a flashlight?"

She picked up the cereal, then handed him the light. "You think it's okay to turn it on?"

"Okay?" Nicholas clapped his hands, enjoying the game in the dark.

Logan grasped her elbow, gently led her down the hall.

"I don't think anyone's outside, but we'll keep the light out for now to be on the safe side."

His agreement melted her frozen heart and lightened her step. Not only had he not belittled her fears, he'd found her concerns worthy of merit. For a moment, she imagined what it would be like to have Logan around on a regular basis. The idea of talking things over and sharing her day with him both frightened and appealed to her. To think such a large, strong man could be so considerate of her opinions left her giddy with a sense of self-worth.

Logan limped beside her, his tone low and intimate in the dark. "Odd how all the other lights in the neighborhood are still on. Have you checked the circuit box?"

"Yes." She thought Logan would head straight for the garage to double-check the panel box, but he seemed to take her word on the matter.

"You *did* pay your electric bill?" his lilting tone teased, and she imagined his smile.

"Very funny."

Nicholas patted her shoulder. "Eat."

She reached into the cereal box and popped a piece of toasted oats into her son's mouth. "What do you think we should check next?"

"Why don't you feed the little guy while I have a look outside?"

She tensed. Now that he was here, she didn't want him to leave. "Do you have to go back out?"

In the dark kitchen, he gave her arm a squeeze of support and encouragement. The scent of his leather jacket mingled with the spicy aroma of soap. "I won't be long. The electricity enters the house on the southwest corner. Lock up behind me."

She sat at the table and fed her son, getting up only to pour milk into Nicholas's plastic straw cup. The few minutes alone in the darkness until Logan knocked again seemed like hours.

He entered with an armload of firewood, and the flashlight tucked between the wood and his chin. With a sharp grunt, he kicked the door shut behind him.

Leaving Nicholas happily eating cereal in his high chair, apparently oblivious to the dark, she eased Logan's burden, taking the flashlight and the top three pieces of wood. "Let me help with that. How's your shoulder?"

"Sore. But if we want the fire to last all night, we need more wood."

He'd said, if *we* want the fire, *we* need more wood. Logan Stone meant to spend the night. Every cell in her body seemed to spring, leaping with tiny electric jolts, as if awakening after a hundred-year sleep.

She shined the flashlight on the far wall of the den, where Logan stacked the firewood into a neat pile beside the fireplace. His powerful hands gripped the split logs with ease, and she imagined his long fingers caressing her shoulders, tracing a tingling path down her back to the sensitive hollow of her waist. When he dusted off his palms and stood, straightening with a catlike grace, she dropped her gaze. What was she thinking? Being carried away by romantic thoughts wasn't like her.

Logan didn't seem to notice her preoccupation. "The wind tossed a tree limb and knocked down the electric wires coming into the house. We can call the power company tonight and hope they'll be out tomorrow, right behind the snowplows."

"Thank goodness." Nearly limp with relief, she rubbed her hands on her arms. So it wasn't some evil stalker trying to kidnap her son. She should have realized it was unlikely that anyone would venture out in this weather. She had to quit jumping to the wrong conclusions and depending on a stranger for help.

Stranger. Logan didn't seem like a stranger anymore, but more like the brother she'd always yearned for. No, that wasn't quite right, either. The feelings she tried so hard to squelch weren't the ones siblings shared, but of close friends, or lovers.

Don't let your thoughts run away with you. She brought herself out of her musing with a harsh shake.

While she stood around daydreaming, Logan needed her help. With his sore shoulder, there was no reason he should carry wood for her. "Why don't you rest. I'll bring in the rest of the wood."

One dark brow lifted. "Give me a minute, and I'll be fine."

Yeah, sure, a moment's rest and his arm would heal good as new. Why did he seem determined to be needed when she was set on managing alone? Perhaps he felt as awkward as she did and needed something to keep him busy? She headed back into the kitchen, took Nicholas out of the high chair and brought him to Logan.

"Can you hold Nicholas for me? There's newspaper and matches in that box." She pointed with the light.

She expected Logan to protest when she wrapped the scarf around her head to go out, but he settled in front of the fireplace with Nicholas. "Come on, pal. Let's build a big fire for your mama."

"Bye-bye?"

"I'll be right back, Nicholas. I'm getting more wood for the fire."

He settled Nicholas between his knees, and her son seemed fascinated with the fireplace.

She liked Logan being so reasonable, liked the fact he wasn't out to prove his strength. Although she couldn't carry as many logs as he did, she could make more trips. But he hadn't pointed out the obvious to build up his macho image like so many men did, and he didn't tell her what to do.

She unlocked the door, and Logan called out, "Watch your footing on the back stoop. It's icy."

She grinned, unable to fault him for voicing one tiny concern. The wind met her at the door and whistled like a pack of circling wolves. Tiny flakes, ever thicker and faster, flurried down and clung to her eyelashes, obscuring her vision. Head down and shoulders hunched against the stinging snow, she trudged through the yard and made four trips to the wood-pile.

On her final trek, he met her at the door with Nicholas over his good shoulder. "Are you frozen?"

The husky concern in his tone, combined with the easy way he held her son over his shoulder, warmed her as she stomped the snow off her shoes. "I'm fine. Can you relock the door?"

She emptied her arms of the last load into the wood bin beside the blazing fire, then took off her jacket. While she'd been outside, Logan had opened the sleep sofa and removed the mattress to the floor in front of the fire. He'd gathered blankets and pillows from the bedroom and piled them into the middle of the mattress in a heap.

Clearly he intended for them to spend the night in front of the fire. The thought kindled a glow inside her that had nothing to do with the crackling flames licking the bark of the oak. She held out her hands to the fire, unwilling to look at him until she regained control of her feelings and forced a semblance of calm into her voice.

Finally she turned to find his gaze riveted on the V-neck opening of her sweater. She glanced down. The wool had slipped down when she'd carried the split logs against her chest, and she'd neglected to straighten the clingy material.

The form-fitting sweater emphasized the gentle swell of her breasts above her nipped-in waistline and hip-hugging jeans. The gleam of interest in Logan's dark eyes and the way her pulse increased in direct response to him set off a silent alarm. She wiped her palms on her thighs. "Are you hungry?"

"Not for food." He tilted his dark head in amusement and devoured her with his eyes.

She didn't dare ask what he was hungry for. The answer was as plain as the passion on his face. Suddenly his ravenous look vanished, replaced by a hardened edge. What had transformed him from romantic to cynic? His sudden change of mood unnerved her, and she blurted, "What are you thinking?"

He didn't answer for so long, she started when he finally spoke in a self-mocking voice. "I'm remembering the last time I wanted a woman."

A woman like you, he implied without saying the words. What had made him so bitter? An explanation might reveal why such a handsome man was still unattached, yet she was not sure she wanted to know more about his romantic past. Fighting her attraction to him was proving more difficult than she'd thought, and, if he gained her sympathy, she might be tempted to make the same mistake she'd made with Joe, fall in love with a man who didn't return her love.

"I give you an opening into my past, and you haven't any questions?"

His direct stare, glinting with challenge, elevated her pulse. She fought to keep her tone steady and ended up sounding much too prim. "Some subjects should remain private."

"Why?"

"Because thinking about the past can be painful," she snapped. He'd prompted her into revealing more than she wished.

"Remaining silent doesn't make the pain go away."

She sucked in her breath at the awful truth. No matter how far she'd run, the memories always followed. She shuddered at her recollections of the coldness that had been her marriage, with Joe's insinuations and his constant put-downs. But although she'd tried to banish her former husband to the tiniest corner of her mind, she couldn't rid herself of the memories that stained her present, eroded her self-esteem. Even from the grave, Joe's warped attitude changed the way she viewed others—even such an obviously fine man like Logan Stone.

Her fingers itched to take the sleeping Nicholas from Logan. Joe had seldom let her near her son, and she still resented it. But Logan was *not* Joe. Logan seemed to want to share part of his past with her, and after all he'd done to help them, the least she could do was listen.

She met his gaze, remembering Ruthie's gossip, recalling how Logan's sister had said a woman broke his heart. "This woman you're remembering—tell me about her."

He handed her the sleeping baby and placed another log on the fire. With one hand, she piled the cushions at the far end of the mattress. Leaning against the pillows, she settled Nicholas in the middle of the blankets, his feet toward the fire.

If Logan noticed she'd placed Nicholas between them, he didn't comment. He kicked off his shoes and stretched back on the mattress; the fire's light glinted off his face.

He spoke in a gentle voice. "I met Allison in New Mexico on the set of a karate film. She had a walk-on part as a hooker." He snorted. "Little did I know how perfect she was for the role."

Tara fiddled with the edge of the blanket. Now that he'd started, she wasn't sure she wanted to hear about this part of his past.

"Between takes, we started talking about stunt work and how the business suddenly had more opportunities for women. When Allison told me she could ride and mentioned her gymnastic background, I encouraged her to become a stunt woman." His self-deprecating laugh couldn't hide his submerged anger.

Turning on her side and resting her cheek in her palm, she studied him. He lay on his back, hands clasped behind his dark hair, and spoke in what seemed a deceptively mild tone. He told his story from behind a suit of emotional armor, resisting all attempts to nick his heart. "Allison learned fast."

"She must have had a good teacher."

"Yeah, right. Her teacher had the right connections. I introduced her to producers and casting directors. Even with my contacts, the work came in slowly at first. But before a month went by, she'd moved into my place.''

He sighed, leaned forward and picked up the poker. He jabbed the logs, and she sensed he was considering how much to tell her. But why should he unburden himself to her? Men didn't usually reveal their inner thoughts easily, especially not to an introvert like her. Men picked outgoing women to talk to, women who were willing to share their thoughts in return.

Sitting up, she drew her knees to her chest and crossed her arms over them, waiting for him to continue.

''Allison never introduced me to her family or friends, and I should have been suspicious, but I was busy with work, and happy when she made a point of entertaining my friends.''

''How long did this go on?''

''Twelve months.''

Twelve months... that's how long she'd been married, and it had seemed like an eternity. But even with Joe's coldness, if she had those months to live again, she wouldn't change a thing. Those months had given her Nicholas.

Logan's silence, and his weighted words about Allison, indicated how much he'd once cared. He might have trouble dealing with his feelings, but unlike Joe, at least he had them. With his back to her, he tended a fire that didn't need his attentions, his shoulders tense, his back stiff. Fiddling with Nicholas's blanket, she waited for the rest of his story.

''Almost two years ago, Allison and I accepted a job together on an action-adventure film. We worked out every detail of the stunt. The car crash should have been safe, but we didn't factor in wind shear.''

''Wind shear?''

''A radical shift in wind speed and direction that occurs over a short distance.''

''Isn't that what makes airplanes crash during landings?'' she asked.

''Yes. It's unpredictable. As we sailed through the air, the sudden gust flipped our car. We landed on the barge upside down. We were lucky.''

''Lucky?''

''The roll bar protected our heads. The shoulder harnesses prevented us from breaking our necks. Allison's head slammed into the car frame, and my knee cracked into the dash. We both ended up in the hospital.'' He took a deep breath and let it out in a long sigh. ''That's when Allison's husband showed up.''

She stared at him. ''Her husband?''

Logan turned toward her, his face inscrutable in shadow, his tone flat. ''Yeah. She'd neglected to tell me she was married.''

Neither his voice nor expression gave a clue to what he was thinking or feeling. But any decent man would be hurting after a woman had so blatantly lied to him. And Logan was more than decent.

Her heart went out to him. ''Was she getting a divorce?''

He dusted imaginary dirt from his hands. ''No. Allison loved him—in her own selfish way. She was using me to advance her career.''

His story had the grainy feel of a nightmare. She didn't know what to say, and her frown deepened. At least he knew why Allison had used him. She'd never understood why Joe had married her. She'd learned too late he'd had no love to give.

From the taut set of Logan's shoulders, she guessed the ambitious woman had hurt him badly. But did he want her pity? She thought not. Or was he still in love with Allison? Was he warning her that he was unavailable?

Her hands picked imaginary pieces of lint from the blanket. "Why did you tell me this?"

He opened his mouth to reply, but the roar of an engine drowned out his voice. Motioning for her to stay with Nicholas, he limped to the window.

But a patchy blackness, bereft of moonlight, made it impossible to see what was going on. By the roar of the engine, Tara guessed the vehicle had driven around the side of the house, across the snowy yard.

She placed her hand on Nicholas's back, then stood. The noise had sent a surge of adrenaline through her, but beside her, her baby didn't stir.

Logan peeked out. "It's a snowmobile."

"Why is it circling my house? What do they want?"

"Get down!" His voice snapped like a whip.

Dropping beside Nicholas, she covered her son with her body and turned anxious eyes to Logan. Who was outside and what did they want?

Dropping into a crouch, Logan hunched down and crawled over to her. "Let's go to the back hallway."

"Why?"

He spoke into her ear. "We're too exposed here." Although he kept his voice down, she sensed the gravity of the situation.

Too exposed to what? Her breath came in shallow gasps. Should they call the police? She strived to keep the fear from her voice. "What did you see out there?"

He shook his head and shrugged. "It's too dark. It could be kids out for a joyride." The urgency in his tone belied his words.

"It's one-thirty in the morning."

"Let's move."

"If we go back there, they might see us through the window."

"If we stay here, we could be hurt. Wrap him in the blankets. Hurry."

Icy anxiety coiled around her spine, clawed her stomach. As the snowmobile circled around the front of the house, Logan picked up Nicholas. "Stay low. Don't give them a target."

She ducked her head, hunched down and scurried across the mattress after Logan. Looking left, right, over her shoulder, she crossed the tile in the kitchen.

Nicholas cried out, fussing at the noise, the movement and the tightly wrapped blanket. "Mama. Mama."

"Mama's right here, darling," she crooned, bumping into Logan's broad back in the dark before skidding to a stop in the hall.

The roar of the snowmobile diminished. For a moment she let herself hope it had gone. Then the engine revved just outside the front. Was someone after her son? Or were neighborhood kids out on a joyride? Did they mean to crash down the front door?

Logan thrust the baby into her arms, turned and zigzagged toward the front of the house. In the dark, the seconds crawled by, and she shifted her weight from foot to foot, wishing Logan hadn't left them alone. A pang of guilt stabbed her conscience. Logan was facing danger to protect her and Nicholas. Again.

Logan shouted from the other end of the house, but she couldn't make out his words, only the tone of his anxious warning, and her stomach clenched. She retreated a step and held her son close.

The blaring engine circled again and approached the front door. A report, sharp as the crack of a rifle, rang out, crashing into the living room.

Chapter Seven

The snowmobile glided into the night, its roar subsiding and leaving behind the crackle of shattered glass that tinkled onto the floor of the dining room. With Nicholas squalling at the top of his lungs in her ear, Tara scurried toward Logan.

"Hush, Nicholas. Don't cry. Mama's here," she murmured, caressing the baby's head, her glance darting back and forth in search of Logan. After that loud boom, she half expected to topple over his prone body on the floor.

"Logan?" She tripped her way into the dining room. "Where are you?"

He yelled from the den. "Stay put. There's glass everywhere."

"Are you hurt?"

"No."

That was hard to believe considering the noise and his location. How could he have avoided the glass? "You're sure you're not hurt?"

"No more than usual," he quipped.

They converged at the dining room's entrance. Logan had retrieved the flashlight from the den and shined the beam on the front wall.

Tara sucked in her breath. The picture window had a hole the size of a baseball in the glass. Around the opening, spiderweb cracks radiated to the window's edge. Snow swished inside, floated onto the cherry dining table and promptly melted.

Logan tilted the light downward and bits of glass glinted across the slate floor. Imagining the tiny slivers slicing flesh, Tara winced, glad they had not been in the room during the attack.

Maneuvering the light back and forth, Logan searched the floor.

She spoke loudly to be heard above Nicholas's cries. "What are you looking for?"

"There!" He held the light steady on an object on the floor.

She slouched, and a numb sense of weariness seeped into her bones. What was happening? All these peculiar incidents could not be mere coincidences. Or could they?

Logan knelt to examine the object. She held back, with a spooky premonition sending a frisson down her spine. "What is it?"

"A rock. We shouldn't touch it and risk disturbing any prints. I'll call Mike, although I don't suppose he'll come out until morning."

She was proud her voice sounded calm although her insides felt like melting gelatin. "Why not?"

"With all this snow, the police are bound to be overworked. The department's understaffed. Unless it's a life-and-death situation, we'll probably have to wait until tomorrow."

Logan shone his flashlight on Tara's tight-pinched face, and her eyes, wide as silver dollars, blinked back fear. He ached to take her into his arms and reassure her. At the same time, his fingers itched to heft the rock and go after whoever was doing this to her. But he didn't dare risk leaving her alone or alarming her further.

"It was probably just some neighborhood kids." He shined the light around the room. Nothing else appeared damaged. "I doubt they'll be back. Go ahead and settle Nicholas by the fire, and I'll see if I can patch this window."

Reaching into his toolbox, he extracted a roll of electrical tape. Crinkling up a wad of newspaper, he stuffed the makeshift patch into the hole in the glass, then taped it into place. The crude repair would prevent the worst drafts until tomorrow, when he'd replace the entire window.

Before he left the dining room, he squatted and inspected the missile. The brown rock, with lots of rough edges, appeared ordinary. Taking prints off it would be tough.

Leaving the stone where it lay, he brushed slivers of glass off the soles of his boots before heading back to the family room. With Nicholas crawling, they needed to take extra precautions.

He returned to the den, and the scent of wood smoke drifted up to welcome him. The fire burned hot, the first logs reduced to fiery embers. Careful not to disturb the baby sleeping in the middle of the mattress, Logan stepped around him and added logs to the fire.

Tara hung up the phone in the kitchen and joined him. "I left a message on Mike's voice mail."

Although she sounded okay, her shoulders were stiff, dark circles lined her eyes, and her face lacked expression—as if she were shell-shocked. She took her place on the far side of the mattress, drew her knees to her chest, and nervously rubbed her shins.

He poked at the fire and gave her time to compose herself. "Are you okay?" He took a seat beside her on the mattress and put his arm over her shoulders, trying to comfort her.

She shoved her hair off her cheek with her palm. "Do you think the same person that tried to take Nicholas threw the rock?"

He shook his head. "It must be a coincidence. A frustrated kidnapper returns to the scene of the crime and hurls a rock through the window? What would be the point?"

"I suppose you're right." She didn't look any more convinced than he felt. "All day, I've jumped to the wrong conclusions. When I woke this morning and Nicholas wasn't in his crib, I thought—"

"Sorry. I didn't mean to frighten you. You were exhausted, and when I heard Nicholas stir, I took him before he woke you."

"And when I found Marge standing over my son in his crib, I thought—"

"Shh," he whispered, consoling her gently. "Don't be so hard on yourself. Thoughts like that are normal after such a scare."

"But I'm seeing threats where none exist. My neighbor, Ruthie, innocently offered to watch the baby and I acted as if she'd like to steal Nicholas away from me. Can you imagine what I was thinking?" Tara shuddered, and he held her tight, wishing he could make all her pain vanish.

They were both seated in front of the fireplace, but its heat provided little comfort. Logan's frustration grew. Tara shouldn't have to stay awake nights worrying that someone could cut off her electricity, throw projectiles through her windows or steal her child. But he'd already said everything he could to reassure her. *Damn it, who was after Nicholas?*

THE NEXT MORNING, Tara awoke with a start to a series of loud bangs. An arm, resting on her shoulder, hampered her movement, and a warm hand cupped her breast. Her back was pressed against Logan's chest, her bottom was curled into his thighs. She was clasping Nicholas to her, and all three of them had slept on their sides like stacked spoons.

Only how had *she* ended up in the middle?

Another thump on the door brought her to her senses, and she scrambled away. The heat of Logan's hand on her breast branded a stamp of guilty pleasure on her conscience.

Stumbling toward the back door, she called out warily, "Who is it?"

"Tara, it's Marge. Is everything all right?"

Too sleepy to think of a good excuse to turn away her inquisitive neighbor, Tara unlocked the door.

Perfectly groomed, Marge had a friendly smile on her ruby lips. "I noticed your lights out last night. Did the electricity fail?"

"A limb fell on the wires coming into the house."

Marge wiped her feet on the mat and entered the kitchen. "I saw smoke billowing out of your chimney, so I figured you wouldn't freeze to death."

In the family room, Nicholas laughed. A thunk from a log being added to the fire carried to the kitchen.

Marge craned her neck toward the den. "Weren't you scared without a man around to help?"

As her gaze sought out the source of the very male chuckle that now accompanied Nicholas's baby coos, her smile faltered. Her eyes narrowed when she took in the mattress in front of the fire and Logan tossing a giggling Nicholas into the air.

Tara was saved from responding when the phone rang. With luck, her nosy neighbor would get bored and disappear. "Excuse me."

Marge waved Tara toward the phone and made herself at home at the breakfast bar.

"Ms. Larson?" the caller asked.

"Yes."

"Bittner here. Our client, Rutherford Everhart, flew in last night, and despite the storm, he must return to Boston today. I need you to show the house on Havenshire Drive to him at one o'clock. Can you swing by the office and read the file? You'll need to familiarize yourself with the listing and pick up the key. I've notified security, and the alarm's been turned off."

She opened a drawer and removed pad and pencil. "That's Rutherford Everhart, at one, on Havenshire Drive. I'll be there."

"I'd see to it myself if my son didn't have a birthday party today. This could be a big sale, so give it your best shot."

She put down the phone, a million details going through her mind. Would the roads be plowed in an hour? If she left, would she miss Detective Scott? And what was she going to do about a baby-sitter?

"Yoo-hoo!" Ruthie poked her head through the door.

Great! Just what she needed, more company.

Marge had made no secret of listening in on Tara's call. "Going somewhere?"

Tara bit her bottom lip. Should she ask Ruthie to watch Nicholas? Or should she take him with her and risk blowing the sale? "I've got to show a house."

"I'll watch Nicholas for you," Logan offered from the den.

Marge and Ruthie exchanged a long look. Marge pouted and Ruthie shrugged.

"Are you sure?" Tara asked him.

"I've got to repair the window and talk to Mike when he gets here." He tossed several logs onto the fire. "And the electric company might need to come inside."

Tara had forgotten all about the electricity. Logan must have fed the fire during the night, since the kitchen and den had remained warm. "Thanks. I shouldn't be long."

Marge snickered. "So you've added baby-sitting to his list of accomplishments. What else have you taught him?'' Her words were obviously meant for Tara, but as she sauntered over to Logan, her hungry gaze never left him.

Tara's smile twitched with amazement. Marge couldn't be real. People just didn't act like this, the stereotypical femme fatale, the brazen hussy, straight out of a grade B movie instead of a Jersey subdivision.

Logan's glare would have frozen the flame off a candle. Marge didn't seem to notice, but Ruthie sent Tara an apologetic look and whispered, ''She's jealous. Hasn't seen her husband since he got her pregnant.''

Marge overheard Ruthie's explanation, burst out crying and threw herself into Logan's arms. Crocodile tears rained down her face. ''I'm so-o-o sorry. The hormones from my pregnancy are making me vile.''

Tara suppressed a grimace. What a show. Marge's theatrical hysterics were forced. Her face didn't turn red when she cried, her eyes weren't puffy, and her nose didn't sniffle. She suspected Marge had contrived to end up exactly where she wanted to be—in Logan's arms.

He extricated himself from her arms round his waist and solicitously guided her to a chair, a concerned look plastered across his face. Tara thought Logan's concern genuine—until he glanced over Marge's head and winked at her.

Most men would have fallen for Marge's performance, but Tara guessed that since he'd grown up with three sisters, he recognized fake hysterics when he saw them. Relieved that Logan had volunteered to baby-sit, she scooped Nicholas off the mattress. "I'll change his diaper before I leave."

"Come back soon." Logan stood and excused himself from Marge and Ruthie, glad to have to call the glass shop and order a window delivered instead of making polite conversation. Next he tried the electric company. He received a busy signal and swore under his breath. Lastly, he called Mike, but had to leave another message.

Ruthie grabbed Marge's arm. "I don't know why I let you talk me into coming over. Tara's managing fine."

Ruthie dragged Marge away with a promise of coffee at her house, which left Logan free to take a quick icy shower in the hall bathroom, brush his teeth and shave. He whistled at his reflection in the mirror, thankful he'd thought to toss a travel kit into his truck after Mike had asked him to look in on Tara.

Snapping the leather kit shut, he studiously ignored the condoms. Tara's neighbors assumed they'd made love, and he wished their accusations had been accurate. His body ached from holding her and letting her sleep.

Last night when she'd wriggled against him, he'd been sure there was no harm in simply cuddling to keep warm. But the sweet scent of her hair enveloped him, and his body responded with an urgency he'd barely controlled. His craving to plant a kiss on the soft spot of her neck nearly overwhelmed him. And when her firm bottom snuggled against his erection, sleep became almost impossible.

He was just helping out his cousin's friend, and he wasn't there to get involved. He couldn't take advantage of her vulnerability. And he wouldn't risk her safety by making sexual advances, since if she refused him, she might feel obligated to send him away despite the danger.

And there *was* danger. He couldn't figure out what the rock through the window had to do with a baby kidnapping, but despite his words to reassure her, he didn't believe in coincidences, either. Only they had no proof, and without proof, they couldn't fight back. Mike couldn't apprehend a suspect. And Nicholas wasn't safe.

Frustrated mentally and physically, he'd lain in the dark, wondering about Tara's past. She'd told him surprisingly little about herself, and he sensed she was hiding something.

He had risen once to feed the fire, then returned to his spot on the mattress, holding her despite the discomfort she caused him. Sometime in the early morning, he'd fallen asleep.

When he'd awakened a few hours after sunrise, he'd been as surprised as she to feel his hand cupping her breast. Small but firm, her breast quivered, and just before she'd pulled away, he'd felt the unmistakable puckering of her nipple pressing into his palm. Had she wanted him as much as he wanted her?

TARA DROVE SLOWLY through the snowy streets, reading her map and scoping out the neighborhood. Luxurious homes, each with privacy fences, sat on five-acre lots. The custom-built homes possessed three-car garages and security systems, and were elegantly landscaped.

The sun was trying and failing to make an appearance through the stormy clouds. Checking her watch, she noted that it was just twelve forty-five.

She pulled into the empty brick drive, pleased the snow had already been plowed. Her prospect hadn't arrived, so she'd have time to explore the house before showing it. Hope swelled in her chest. If she could make this sale, she and Nicholas would have a cushion to fall back on from a hefty commission.

Stepping out of the car, she barely noticed the chill. Her gaze took in the trimmed hedges, the cherry tree in the front yard, the huge skylights in the steeply pitched cedar roof.

Her interest dropped from the roof to the wide eaves, then to one of the imposing stained-glass front doors that stood open wide to the cold.

Her neck prickled. Now what? Common sense told her not to enter the house. Anyone could be inside. But then maybe it was only that the last person to show the house had forgotten to lock the door. Or perhaps the wind had simply blown the door open.

Should she check with a neighbor? She looked east and west for a sign of activity. Her best bet would be to go across the street, ask if they'd seen anything unusual. But without interior lights shining or the driveway shoveled, that house appeared vacant.

She would have preferred to leave, but her obligation was to stay and warn her client. Otherwise, the client could arrive, walk into the house looking for her and come face-to-face with a possible burglar.

Her stomach clenched. She paced beside her car, reached in and leaned on the horn, hoping the noise would attract someone to her presence or scare an intruder inside the house into leaving by a back door. The blare sent two crows soaring out of the cherry tree, and several squirrels scolded her from the roof.

Reluctant to approach the house, she waited thirty long, cold minutes in the drive. When no one showed, she edged her way to the front door and shouted, "Anybody home?"

Nothing but silence.

No matter how badly she wanted to get away, she couldn't leave the house open to vandals. With a quick flick of her arm, she reached inside, yanked the door shut and locked it. Spinning on her heel, she sprinted to the car.

AFTER MIKE HAD COME BY and collected the rock, Logan directed the men from the power company to the problem the fallen tree limb had created. He and Nicholas shared a cold breakfast of milk and cereal, and by the time they'd finished, power had been restored.

The plate glass would never have arrived the same day he'd ordered it if he hadn't given the glass company a huge order last summer. With Nicholas zipped in his jacket, strapped in his high chair and biting a plastic truck, Logan knocked the pieces of shattered glass through the dining room window, swept the slivers off the floor and vacuumed. The room's temperature dropped, and while he stripped the old caulking from the window frame, he kept a close eye on the baby.

For once, his timing couldn't have been better. He finished just as the glass truck arrived, and the men helped him set the pane in place while the baby watched from his stroller.

When he finished, he carried Nicholas back into the house, settled on the couch, kicked off his boots and put the baby on the floor.

With a hopeful grin, Nicholas crept over to him, climbed into his lap and pointed to a stack of books. "Read."

Logan chuckled. "At last, someone who wants to listen to me."

"Read?"

"Okay." He plucked the book off the top of the stack. "Once upon a time, there was a mama bear, a daddy bear—"

"Da-da?" Nicholas twisted and patted his chin.

He ruffled the kid's hair. "I'm not a daddy. Maybe someday. I'd like a kid like you." Although Nicholas couldn't possibly understand his explanation, when Logan resettled him in his lap, he didn't protest. "And there was a baby bear."

Halfway through the story, Nicholas fell asleep, his head resting in the crook of Logan's arm. "Tired you out, did I?"

For some reason, Logan was reluctant to put him in his crib. Never before had he known the joy of holding a child. With three sisters, there had always been a female around to pick up his nieces and nephews. Until now, he hadn't realized what he'd been missing.

He'd closed himself off for so long, he'd forgotten what it was like to feel close to anyone. Although he'd shut himself off from risk and pain, he'd shut out the happy moments, too.

Outside, a car pulled into the drive. Logan carried the baby to his room and eased Nicholas into his crib, handed him his well-worn dinosaur and covered him with a blanket. Straightening, he walked to the front door and opened it.

Tara climbed the stoop, her face white, her lips trembling.

Logan sensed her tension and knew something terrible had transpired. After all she'd been through, a rush of sympathy coursed through him, knowing that something else had gone wrong. Stepping outside, he clasped her arm. "What's wrong? What happened?"

Her head dipped, and she covered her face with her hands. "I was fired!"

While he wished for a way to ease her concerns, his arms encircled her, gathering her to him until her head rested against his chest. For her to be so upset when she could find another job, something out of the ordinary must have occurred. "Maybe I can help," he whispered, stroking back the silken strands of hair that clung to her cheek. "Tell me what happened."

Trembling against him, she snuggled closer. "I didn't do anything wrong. I picked up the file and key from the office. When I arrived at the property, no one was there. The front door was wide open."

She could have been in danger, and if someone had been there before her, the house could have been robbed. He tightened his hold, but then forced his hands to relax and cradle her, rocking gently. "You didn't go inside, did you?"

She shook her head, and her perfume drifted to him on the fresh air. "I thought burglars might be there. I waited half an hour for the client. When he didn't show, I locked the door and returned to the office.''

Her trembling increased, and he braced for the worst. "Then what happened?"

Her head snapped up, and she looked straight at him, outrage on her face. "Mr. Bittner accused me of meeting and propositioning my client. He said the man was highly offended. Not only did we lose the sale, he's threatening to sue me for incompetence and loss of the sale.''

He stared down at her, dumbfounded that anyone could accuse her of propositioning a stranger. This was the woman who had hesitated to let him, her best friend's cousin, sleep on her couch. This was the woman who had gone out of her way to avoid touching him when she tucked an afghan over his lap. The idea of her coming on to a stranger was asinine, and the accusation angered him.

For her sake, he thrust his anger aside. Right now, she needed compassion. Logan's arms came up and his hands massaged the tight muscles of her neck, and he forced himself to speak calmly. "Did you tell Bittner you never met the buyer?"

"He called me a liar. And then he checked and found out I was fired from my last job.''

"You were?" Her revelation surprised him. He couldn't imagine her as anything but efficient, competent and loyal, an employee a broker would be lucky to have.

She pulled away, anger flaring in her eyes. "My last boss told me I was let go due to an office cutback, but I found out differently." Her voice shook with outrage. "Conrad Pemberton had me fired."

Her color returned to normal, and he continued to rub her neck and shoulders, wishing he could ease her anguish as easily as tense muscles. But her words had left him puzzled. "How could he arrange that unless you worked for him?"

She shook her head, but didn't pull away from his arms. "Conrad's very influential. He suggested he'd throw some business to the firm if they let me go, and they were more than eager to do his bidding. That's why I moved here—to stay out of his reach." She let out a shaky laugh. "I guess my plan didn't work."

No wonder she'd suspected Conrad was behind the kidnapping. Standing up to her father-in-law must have been a nightmare. The thought of her alone and working, trying to protect her son while Pemberton sought to have her dismissed, made him wish the man would show up so Logan could confront him. "Do you think he set you up again?"

"Anything's possible. He's called here, and we had another argument about Nicholas."

He tried to keep his tone level. Right now, Tara needed someone to help her, someone with a clear head. If her father-in-law had been there, Logan's first reaction would have been a strong right fist to Pemberton's jaw. But her father-in-law was out of reach, probably gloating in his executive suite, and she was in his arms, needing someone to believe in her. "Why would Conrad bother to get you fired?"

"So I'd go begging to him for money."

"But you won't."

Her fingers clenched his shirt. "Never."

As she voiced her determination, his heart thumped erratically. The woman had spunk and he admired her for it. He smoothed back her hair, running his fingers through the lustrous strands. "If he's smart, he knows you won't give in."

With her head tilted back, she stared at him, her face full of questions and uncertainties. "If I'm broke, he could petition the court for custody."

As if struck by a blow, Logan shuddered. Hadn't she been through enough? He held her closer, wishing desperately he could spare her the anguish.

He yearned to hold and protect her forever from all that threatened her. Gathering her closer, and with a soft groan, he kissed her. All at once she leaned into him, her breasts pressed to his chest, her hips wedged against him, creating a fierce all-consuming need for more.

Carried away by his response, Logan almost failed to hear a car stopping in front of the house. When a car door opened, he finally pulled back.

Her face had lost its pallor and sported a healthy glow. The smoldering flame in her eyes kindled a fire inside him that would never be satisfied with just one kiss. If it weren't for the intrusion, he'd have been tempted to sweep her into his arms, carry her across the threshold and spend the afternoon making love, blotting out all her fears and worries with his touch.

Reluctantly, he turned his attention to the stretch limousine at the curb. She did the same and gasped. Her knees buckled, and he took a firm grasp of her arm to steady her.

An older gentleman in a fedora and cashmere overcoat strolled up the sidewalk, his arms full of stuffed animals and a bouquet of helium balloons. The driver opened the back of the limo and unloaded cartons into the snow.

Tara's healthy flush disappeared. She placed her hands on her hips, stiffened her shoulders, raised her chin. "I can't believe *he* has the nerve to come here."

Chapter Eight

"Who the hell is he?" Logan asked.

Cold dignity created a stony mask on Tara's face. "That's Conrad Pemberton, my former father-in-law."

Stooped from carrying a multitude of stuffed animals, Conrad appeared feeble. Logan's earlier ire and his wish to plant his fist on Pemberton's jaw receded. He would be ashamed of himself to strike a man of his advanced age.

Conrad stopped before them, raked Logan with a scowl and promptly ignored him. He looked through his glasses and down his long nose at Tara. "So now you're carrying on with Hollywood riffraff?"

How could Pemberton have known he worked in Hollywood unless he'd had him investigated? Was Pemberton secretly watching the house and waiting for another opportunity to kidnap Nicholas? But then why show up in broad daylight on Tara's doorstep?

Her voice stayed cool. "What I do is no concern of yours."

"Your behavior reflects on my grandson. His mother shouldn't be cavorting in the streets with the hired help."

Logan held his temper in check. So the old man knew why he was here, and he'd seen their kiss. So what?

But why did Pemberton hold Tara in such low regard?

Logan crossed his arms across his chest and remained silent. If Pemberton kept talking, perhaps he might slip up and implicate himself in the attempted kidnapping. Besides, Tara needed a chance to stand up to Pemberton, something she probably hadn't done while her husband was alive. He wouldn't be helping her by fighting her battles for her.

Tara didn't back down. "What do you want?"

"I've brought a few presents for my grandson."

"And you want to see what kind of house he lives in?" Her voice dripped shards of ice.

Pemberton held her stare, but he was the first to look away. "I'm Nicholas's grandfather. He's all I have left."

Logan suspected those simple words were as close as the old man would ever come to begging. What had caused such a rift between them that they couldn't communicate without innuendos, scowls and ugly accusations? While he didn't see the harm in letting Conrad spend a few supervised minutes with Nicholas, the decision was hers. Whatever she decided, he'd back her up.

Conrad's plea softened her hard glare. She swept her arm wide toward the door. "Come in. I have nothing to hide."

She led Conrad to the baby's room, and Logan headed toward the den. He'd folded the mattress back into the sofa before they joined him in tense silence.

Conrad's sharp-eyed glance took in the folded blankets and pillows from the night spent together in front of the fire, but he didn't comment. Maybe he assumed only Logan had slept there, but Logan doubted he'd be that generous in his thoughts toward Tara.

Conrad didn't ask to hold his grandson. Instead he placed the stuffed animals on a low table and waited for Nicholas's reaction.

The kid's face lit up with delight and he crawled to the teddy bear. "Mine?"

Conrad nodded and his glasses slipped on his nose. "For you."

On the surface, the tension between Tara and Conrad seemed to ease. Yet Logan sensed a dark undercurrent of emotion, old hurts, old pain. What had caused Pemberton's animosity toward Tara?

The limo driver entered the room with two cartons. "Where do you want the computer set up, sir?"

Tara shook her head. "Nicholas is too young for a computer."

Using the coffee table for leverage, her son drew himself upright and toddled to the boxes. "Mine?"

Conrad cleared his throat. "It's about time he started walking."

"Walking and talking aren't done on a schedule. Nicholas will do things in his own time."

"I want him to have every advantage. He should be exposed to music, art, the classics."

Tara sighed in obvious frustration. Logan leaned against the breakfast bar and decided it was time to intervene, even if it was presumptuous. "You raised your son the way you saw fit. Now it's Tara's turn."

"Who asked you?"

"Your grandson is healthy and well-fed. He has a loving and caring mother."

"That's not enough. He's a Pemberton, and by God—" Conrad whacked his hand on the arm of the couch "—he doesn't belong in an ordinary subdivision with a working mother who will stick him in day care."

Tara stood, her voice calm, but Logan noticed her hands shaking. "I think it's time you left."

"I'll leave when I'm good and ready, young lady. I didn't drive all this way—"

Logan uncoiled from his spot by the breakfast bar and placed himself between Tara and her father-in-law. "This is her home. You'll leave now, Mr. Pemberton."

"You're making a mistake. I'll take her to court and sue for custody."

Logan shrugged. "It won't do you any good. Millions of women work and leave their children in day care."

"She's irresponsible to leave a child with a Hollywood pervert. She doesn't even have a job. She sleeps with strangers."

"My life is none of your business," Tara snapped. "How dare you come into my house and accuse me of anything?"

Exasperation and anger tightened her mouth, but without another word she picked up Nicholas and walked out of the room.

Logan jerked the old man by his coat. "What's wrong with you, Pemberton? What kind of man would try to separate a mother from her son?"

The limo driver entered with three more boxes. "Did you decide where you want me to put these?"

"Right there—" Logan pointed to a corner of the den "—will be fine. Mr. Pemberton's visit is over." Keeping a firm grip on the old man's arm, Logan escorted him out the door, and the driver followed.

In the bedroom Tara changed Nicholas's disposable diaper. Thank goodness she didn't have to deal with safety pins. Her hands shook so hard she would have jabbed his tender skin for sure.

While she was glad Conrad was gone, she couldn't help berating herself. It should have been her, not Logan, who escorted her father-in-law to the door. Maybe if Logan hadn't been so bold, she might have found the courage to kick Conrad out herself. Then again, maybe not. She should appreciate Logan jumping to her defense, but after months of new-found independence, she hated depending on a man.

Why couldn't Conrad leave them alone? He knew just how to get to her. She should never have let him in the house. But she'd thought with Logan there he would at least be civil, and she'd also hoped he might slip up and mention the kidnapping attempt. She should have known he was too smart for that.

She would have loved to accuse him of having her fired from her new job. But she'd kept her mouth shut, unwilling to accuse him without proof.

"Nicholas, hold still." She snapped the leggings over his diaper, carried him to her room and sat him in the middle of the floor, where he played with a plastic book while she changed from business clothes to jeans and a sweater.

When she emerged, Nicholas in her arms, Logan was standing in front of the fireplace. Although the propane was back on, she appreciated the fire. The cheery, crackling blaze flickered over Logan's stoic features as he closed the glass doors screening the flames. She set Nicholas down, and he promptly crawled over to his new toys. Tara joined him and examined each stuffed animal with care. She removed a ribbon from around the neck of a bear, and when Nicholas looked the other way, she confiscated a giraffe and zebra.

"Is something wrong with those toys?" Logan asked.

"I'm just careful. These have buttons for eyes, and Nicholas might pluck them out. Everything still goes into his mouth."

What a good mother she was, careful, concerned, loving. Instead of complaining and threatening, Pemberton should be grateful she took such good care of his grandchild.

The phone rang. "I'll get it," Logan offered.

Tara leaned her head back on the couch and closed her eyes. She didn't want to talk to anyone right now. Between losing her job and sparring with Conrad, she was exhausted, more than willing to let Logan deal with the phone call.

"I'm not surprised you couldn't get prints," she heard him say.

That must be Mike. She hadn't yet had time to ask Logan what Mike had said this morning when he'd come by. Apparently, the rock was another dead end. But right now, she was too fatigued to worry.

"Tara has several nosy neighbors. Why not run a check on Marge Henley and Ruthie Raines? Thanks, Mike." She heard the phone click in its cradle.

Tara's eyes jerked open. Nicholas had crawled over to Logan, and he scooped up her son. They looked right together, the giant of a man holding her giggling child so tenderly. She swallowed a sigh, knowing the situation could never be permanent.

"Did Mike discover anything new?"

"The rock didn't have even a smudged print. But the glove on the back stoop was made by the same shop Pemberton frequents."

She hoisted herself onto the couch. "The style and glove size?"

"Match Pemberton's purchases. But a glove is not enough evidence. Even if Mike could prove the glove is your father-in-law's, it only indicates he might have been here—not that he tried to take Nicholas."

"So now what? We just wait until he tries again?"

"I'm not sure he's guilty. You said yourself Pemberton's not the kind of man to break and enter. A man of his stature is more likely to go to court and use his influence to sway a judge. That's why I suggested checking out the neighbors."

"But why would you suspect them?"

"Everyone's a suspect until they're proven innocent. Ruthie is too interested in Nicholas. And I don't like the way Marge lets herself into the house."

She hesitated, wondering if she was being rational. "Shouldn't you and I have discussed having Mike investigate them?"

"Why?"

"Mike should be watching Conrad." She tried to keep the bite out of her tone, but Logan must have picked up on her irritation.

He carried Nicholas to the couch and took a seat beside her. "Your neighbors will never know Mike is investigating them. What can it hurt?"

Despite her resolution to remain strong, her voice quavered. "I want to make my own decisions, and it seems like you're taking over."

Nicholas wriggled out of Logan's lap and sat at their feet, tugging on the ears of a stuffed elephant.

Logan put two fingers beneath her chin and tilted her head to look at him. Their gazes locked. "If you want, I'll call Mike back and tell him how you feel."

How could she stay angry with a man so considerate of her feelings? A gratifying warmth flowed through her, and she leaned into him. "You did the right thing. I'm overly sensitive when it comes to someone making decisions for me. Joe didn't . . . give me enough room."

Logan's hand caressed the side of her neck and sent shooting tingles of pleasure through her. It felt so good *not* to be alone, to have someone to share her problems.

"You don't like to talk about him, do you?" Logan asked.

She wanted the memories of her dead husband behind her. Laying her head on Logan's shoulder, she watched her son and smiled. "Nicholas was the only good thing to come out of that marriage."

"At least something good came of it."

She heard the bitterness in his tone and recalled the reason for it. Nothing good had come from his relationship with Allison. Tara couldn't imagine a married woman pretending to fall in love just to advance her career. Logan hadn't had much luck with women, yet he'd been so open about his difficulties.

"Why did you tell me about Allison?"

Logan took her hand in his callused one. "Since Allison, I've kept my distance from women. But with you . . . it's different. I haven't felt the way I do about you . . . ever before. I thought we should go slow. And I didn't want you to think I would take advantage of your situation."

A tightness she'd carried around for a year loosened, as if a tremendous burden had suddenly lifted. With Logan, she could discuss her problems like an adult. She could argue with him and he wouldn't treat her with days of cold silence. And this freedom to have a choice lightened a weight in her heart. Twisting in his lap, she wound her hands around his neck and into his thick hair, and raised her lips to his.

A smile twitched the corner of his mouth, and he required no further invitation. Unlike their first tender kiss, this one was hot, hard, hungry. His scent enveloped her in a heated cloud, as dizzying as the heights of a starlit sky, or a resplendent summer sunrise.

"Mama." Nicholas tugged on her sweater.

Breathless, she broke away from him. "What, sweetie?"

"Eat."

She stood to put some distance between her and Logan. His mouth turned up with pleased amusement as if he knew their kiss had sent her emotions reeling.

"What would you like for supper?" she asked Logan.

"You." His eyes shone with a wicked gleam.

His words shot a surge of sizzling heat straight to her heart. It would be so easy to fall in love with him.

Nicholas yanked on her jeans. "Eat. Eat."

She laughed at his impatience and the welcome distraction. "How about spaghetti?"

"Sketti," Nicholas mimicked.

"Fine," Logan agreed. A teasing smile twitched his lips. "As long as I get Mama for dessert."

Lord, he was tempting. Wrapped in his embrace, she could forget the past, the problems of the present. But now that she was no longer in his arms, she had to wonder if they could have a future.

She put her hands on her hips. "I thought you said you wanted to go slow?"

He arched a brow. "Is that what you want?"

She disengaged Nicholas from her jeans and turned on her heel, no longer able to stand her ground and face him. "You have me so dizzy, I don't know what I want."

Chuckling, he spoke to her back. "You know exactly what you want. You just haven't admitted it to yourself."

Could he read her thoughts? Heat rose in her cheeks. She couldn't turn around or he'd see the blush of pink that must be staining her face. She retreated to the kitchen, her emotions unbalanced, as if she were walking on a thin, high wire. He'd said he wanted to go slow, and then he'd kissed her with a fire that had almost raged out of control.

Thawing a package of homemade sauce in the microwave, she thought of the last time a man had made her feel this excited, about two years ago, when Joe had just proposed and she'd thought she was the luckiest woman alive. She'd accepted his proposal and made the worst mistake of her life.

He'd put her through hell, and she had yet to set her life back in order. She'd need more time to be ready for a man like Logan Stone.

And how often will a man like him walk into your life? She opened a box of spaghetti and broke pieces into a pot of boiling water.

Stirring the pasta, she recalled everything Logan had done for her. He'd risked his life to save her son. He'd driven through a snowstorm to make sure she and Nicholas were all right. And he kissed like a hot dream on a steamy summer night.

She couldn't deny she wanted him. Why not allow herself the pleasure he wanted to give? Over these last months, she'd grown stronger, but during the past few days with Logan, she'd come to think she might once again trust her judgment.

Logan Stone was nothing like Joe. Where Joe was cold and a bully, Logan was considerate and thoughtful. And she couldn't let the doubts and insecurities from her former marriage embitter the rest of her life. She refused to spend her days wary of happiness, frightened of intimacy.

And she'd changed, too. Her determination not to repeat the mistakes of her past would make it difficult for any man to undermine her confidence. Never again would a man intimidate her into following his wishes.

Not that Logan would ever act so coldly. Deep in her heart, she knew he would discuss, not coerce; ask, not demand. And she couldn't forever live in fear of making another mistake.

But if she was going to share her heart, her body, shouldn't she be willing to share her past?

She fed Nicholas first, and Logan offered to put him to bed while she set the table and made a salad. When Logan returned and set the baby monitor with its new set of batteries on the kitchen counter, she'd already dimmed the lights and lit a candle.

He pulled out her chair, then took the seat across from her. "That looks great. Are we celebrating something?"

With what she hoped was a provocative smile, she raised her wineglass. "To our first night."

Logan leaned back, stretched his legs out in front of him and regarded her from beneath half-lowered lids. His mouth curled in a faint smile that didn't alter the interested watchfulness in his eyes. "You're sure?"

She nodded, suddenly unable to meet his gaze. Her heart thumped erratically. Her mouth went dry at the thought of making love. "Yes."

Clinking her glass with his, she licked her bottom lip nervously. Meeting his eyes over the rim of her glass, she took a sip and soothed her parched throat, but nothing could cool the heat he'd kindled inside her. Her expression must have revealed her desire, her need to trust him.

His brows lifted in amazement. "So you've decided to tell me about Joe?"

She nodded, set down her glass and played with the stem. "Right from the beginning, I wondered why Joe picked me."

"Why?"

She loved him for asking, for insinuating how natural loving her seemed. "I didn't fit into his life-style with the lavish parties, old-world ties and Ivy League connections. For the first time in my life, I put aside my belief that happy endings were nothing more than a child's fairy tale. I dared to dream my Prince Charming had come to sweep me away to his castle."

She twirled the wineglass by its stem and flashed him a wry smile. "The day after we married, the prince turned into a toad."

He chuckled sympathetically. "Had you known him long before you married?"

"A year." She sighed. "But five years wouldn't have been enough. Joe could have won an Oscar for his acting ability. Before we married, he convinced me he loved me. Afterward, he had the world fooled into believing he was a warm father, a loving husband. But after I got pregnant, he never touched me again. We didn't make love. He didn't kiss me. He wouldn't hold my hand."

"Why?"

"I don't know. He was obsessed with my pregnancy. He watched every spoonful I ate. He wouldn't let me go outside if it rained. I humored him, thinking once Nicholas was born, our lives would take on a more normal tone."

Logan studied her. "It sounds like you were a prisoner."

"In a way, I was. I didn't want to displease Joe. When I did, he quit talking to me. Sometimes he didn't speak for days. It's a wonder Nicholas turned out to be such a happy baby. I was tense throughout the entire pregnancy."

"What happened after Nicholas was born?"

Her insides tightened, rolled and wound into a knot. "Joe never let me near my son. He didn't even want me to breast-feed. He insisted I return to work a week after Nicholas arrived, and he took over the baby's care."

"He sounds...strange." His tone was laced with censure. But she wasn't surprised by the compassion in his gaze.

"Joe told me I wasn't a good mother. When I held Nicholas he would take him away and claim I upset him. If I fed or bathed Nicholas, Joe hovered over me as if I would drop him."

"That kind of treatment would cause any new mother to question her competency."

Tara nodded, glad he understood. "I began to feel unsure of myself. I thought of leaving, but he would have fought me for custody, and with Joe's connections, I was afraid I'd lose Nicholas forever."

Logan's mouth drew into a bleak line. "He was intimidating you. But why?"

"I don't know." She inhaled a shuddering breath. "The scary thing is that when someone puts you down, someone who supposedly loves you, you begin to believe him. I suppose I'll never know why Joe did what he did. If he thought I wasn't good enough to be the mother of his son, why did he marry me?''

"Good question."

"And one which I'll never know the answer. He was killed in a boating accident when Nicholas was one month old. For a long time, I saw Joe's face in my dreams." She shuddered. "Sometimes I'd see someone that looked like him in the park, on the street, and I wanted to run to that man and ask him why? Why did he treat me so badly? But, of course, he wasn't Joe."

Logan reached across the table, took her hand and rubbed his thumb along her palm. "And the hard part is that you'll never have an answer. You'll always wonder if you did something or said something to make him treat you the way he did."

She smiled sadly. "Thanks for understanding. And you'll understand why tonight is difficult for me, even though I want us to be together."

"You might come to trust me in time."

"Trusting you isn't the problem." She spoke adamantly. "After I made such a terrible mistake, how can I trust myself?"

"For one thing, you're older. And for another, you're wiser." Rising, he drew her away from the table and into his arms. His lips caressed her ear, and she shivered with pleasure. When he pulled back and stared down at her with a tender gleam, his mouth quirked in amusement. "And last but not least, I'm going to change your mind."

"Really?"

"Convincing you to believe in yourself is going to be my personal challenge." His eyes twinkled in the candlelight, then his head dipped for a kiss.

She stood on tiptoe, rising to meet him halfway. He planted tiny kisses across her brow, nibbling her cheek, lightly nipping her lips. Her fingertips dug into the bulge of muscles at his shoulders. Pulling him closer, she guided his lips to hers and sipped and savored a bursting bouquet of red wine.

Slipping his hand under her sweater, he cupped her breast. She inhaled sharply at the contact, her whole body vibrating with new life, then she broke their kiss, her lips parting in a small gasp.

His eyes glinted with pleasure. "Do you like this?"

"Umm." The pads of his thumbs circled her nipples through her silk bra. Her flesh puckered immediately under his touch, and she let out a breathy sigh. Joe had never cared enough to try to please her. With him, the sexual act had been cold, remote, mechanical.

But Logan's hands were warm and excitingly masculine. He instinctively knew what she liked, and he wasn't in a hurry to move on to his own pleasure. Deftly, he unhooked her bra. The heat of his palms against her bare flesh sent exquisite shivers racing along her neck.

He seemed to react to her tiniest tremors, taking his cues from her response, prolonging the pleasure, his palms circling her breasts in languid caresses until her legs felt as if they'd turned to water and she could barely stand.

Shimmers of delight swooped from her breasts to her belly. Her hands glided to his chest, steadying her.

Her fingers fumbled with buttons, and shoved flannel back to reveal a triangle of chest hair sweeping across an expanse of solid muscles and dipping to a point that disappeared beneath his belt buckle.

While her fingers explored the heated flesh of his chest, he removed her sweater and bra. Before she could satisfy the urge to unfasten his belt, he swept her into his arms, carried her into the den and set her down on a thick rug in front of the fire.

He lay on his side next to her, the fire's light reflecting off his skin and highlighting a jagged scar below his collarbone and another by his elbow. She leaned forward, pressing him onto his back, and kissed his neck where his pulse beat fast enough to match her racing heart. She dipped her head lower, letting the length of her hair trail along his chest, tickling and taunting.

He hissed and fumbled for her zipper, but she wriggled away, intent on her exploration. Her tongue found the valley of his stomach, and her fingers unbuttoned his jeans. Impatiently, he sat up and kicked them off along with his boxer shorts.

She glanced below his waist, and her blood quickened at how ready he was for her. Kneeling, she leaned into him, eager for another taste of his lips. His hands clasped her waist, allowing only her bare nipples to touch his chest. It felt heavenly, and she let out a soft moan.

Still keeping a slight distance between them, he nuzzled her ear with his lips, his hands working their magic on her breasts. "Do you like this?"

"Mmm." How was it possible to set her entire body on fire when he'd only touched one small part of her flesh? He'd kindled a blaze that spread like wildfire. But he hadn't touched just one small part of her. He'd lit up her soul and enflamed her heart.

Her blood pulsed faster than a shooting star. She closed her eyes and inhaled his musky scent, her fingers grazing the cords of muscles along his shoulders. "You feel so good."

His husky whisper against her lips taunted her. "Tell me what you want."

"Kiss me," she demanded.

"Where?"

Her eyes flew open in surprise. She took in the hunger in his gaze and dared to voice a secret wish. With this man, she could dare to fly. "Everywhere."

After slipping off her jeans and panties, he positioned her close to the fire. His lips burned a path from her mouth, to her neck, to her breast. As he gave equal attention to her other breast, her back arched, her fingers slid into his hair.

Slowly, sensuously, his tongue searched out the sensitive spot by her hip, lapped her navel and dipped lower. Her thighs parted, and her fingers clenched the carpet. As searing, sizzling fire licked her, every muscle drew taut.

He paused for a moment, and she heard him digging through his clothing, ripping open a package.

"Let me do that," she said boldly, wanting this first time with him to experience every pleasure together.

She took her time, exploring him with her fingers, teasing him unmercifully. She loved the way his eyes hooded with fiery passion, adored his soft groan when she found an especially sensitive spot.

"Woman, if you don't hurry, we'll both be disappointed."

She reveled in the notion she could affect him like that. The moment she finished her task, he kneeled between her thighs.

When he entered her, she wrapped her legs around him, drawing him closer. His hands cupped her buttocks. His breath came in quick gasps.

"Sorry, darling. I can't wait."

His mouth found hers, and he was over her, inside her. With one last deep thrust of fierce fury, he rocketed her to the stars and her thoughts scattered to the ends of the cosmos.

She regained her senses slowly, languorous satisfaction seeped from every pore, and she basked in the remembrance of the unbridled fury he'd been unable to contain. He'd rolled over, taking her with him, so they now lay on their sides.

His hand came up to brush aside her hair. "I wanted you so badly, I couldn't hold back. Give me a few minutes and next time will be better."

A warm thrill washed through her. To think that he could want her so badly that he'd lost control made her suppress a happy grin. She didn't know if she could ever get enough of him. "Thank you."

"For what?"

"For giving me so much pleasure."

He brushed a lock of hair from her forehead and kissed her shoulder. "The feeling's mutual."

Then he made love to her again.

WHEN TARA AWOKE, it was to the scent of cold ashes swirling in the grate and a sooty taste on her lips. Despite the stimulating evening, she was awake at her usual hour, but she didn't hear a sound on the baby monitor.

Tiptoeing to avoid waking Logan, she hurried to the bedroom. Nicholas was usually up by now. Odd she hadn't heard his crib springs creak or the pleasing little cooing sounds he made as he played with his toys.

She opened the door. Logan had drawn the curtains closed and put Nicholas's crib in the far corner just in case another rock came through a window. Why wasn't he awake? Could he be cutting another tooth and running a fever?

She edged nearer to the crib. Slowly her eyes adjusted to the darkness. The mobile hanging from the ceiling rustled against her face, and she batted it away. The black outlines of a blanket in the corner of his mattress sluggishly took shape. But it wasn't a big-enough silhouette to cover her son.

Her heart heaved into her throat, and she couldn't breathe. Nausea churned in her stomach. Flicking on the light, she stared at her son's empty crib.

Nicholas was gone.

Chapter Nine

"Nicholas!"

Tara rushed to the empty crib and tossed the blanket onto the floor. She wheeled around and her knees buckled, toppling her into Nicholas's dresser. She yanked herself upright and, frantic for the sight of him, darted a glance across the bedroom and down the hall. Could he have climbed out of his crib?

"Nicholas!"

She checked her room, behind the curtains, jerked open the closet door to find nothing but empty floor space and boxes stacked against the far wall. Nothing. Dashing into the bathroom, she ripped the shower curtain aside, threw open the cabinet and peered under the sink.

Logan pounded down the hall. Outside her bedroom, they almost collided. He steadied her, his expression grim. "What's wrong?"

Her voice rose an octave. "Nicholas is gone."

Logan's face went white, and his lips tightened. He grabbed her arms. "Are you sure?"

"Of course I'm sure!"

Logan pulled her close in a gesture that let her know he shared her distress. "Let's try to stay calm. Where have you looked?"

"His room and mine."

"I'll check the extra bedroom and bath. You look in the dining room and kitchen."

Tara reeled away, anxious tears spilling from her eyes. One glance into the empty dining room and she sprinted toward the kitchen. *Be there, Nicky. Please, be there.* But the empty, gleaming tile of the cheery kitchen mocked her.

"See if the back door is locked," Logan yelled from the other room.

Numb, Tara twisted the knob, but the door didn't budge. She tried the garage door, and it, too, was locked.

Logan dashed back to the kitchen. "The front door is open, but I locked it after Conrad left. Call Mike. Every second makes a difference."

She stumbled to the phone, her hands shaking so badly she could barely dial. Someone picked up on the first ring.

"Harden Police Department."

"Detective Scott, please." Tara's fingers gripped the phone, her trembling fingers. "Hurry. This is an emergency."

"Detective Scott isn't here. May I help you?"

"My baby, Nicholas, has been kidnapped."

"Ma'am, when did you last see the child?"

"When we put him to bed, around eight."

"How old is he?"

"Eleven-and-a-half months."

"What was he wearing?"

"A yellow sleeper with booties."

After Tara described Nicholas's hair and eye color and gave them her address, the officer spoke in a soothing tone. "Just relax, ma'am. We'll send an officer right out and issue an alert."

She hung up the phone and, with Logan, searched the house again, but found no trace of Nicholas. "If only I'd slept in my room last night, I might have heard something," she sobbed. "If I hadn't been so distracted..."

Logan patted her shoulder. "It's not your fault. There's nothing more you could have done to keep Nicholas safe. If you tied him to you on a leash, he'd grow up neurotic."

"Better neurotic than missing," she snapped and pulled away from his attempt to calm her.

His words couldn't ease the guilt stabbing her. If they hadn't made love, she wouldn't have slept so soundly, wouldn't have been so far away from her son, might have prevented his disappearance.

Logan tried to take her into his arms. "You're not thinking clearly."

"Don't tell me how to think!" She yanked free of his grip.

"We'll find him. You've got to believe that."

"Why? Kids disappear all the time." Her voice broke, then continued in a whisper, "And no one ever hears from them again."

Once more, he tried to embrace her, but she brushed him off. "Don't. Not now."

He backed away, concern darkening his eyes. "Take it easy."

But she didn't want his pity, or his touch. She'd taken her own pleasure with Logan and made love, putting her son at risk. Guilt gnawed at her until her stomach churned. If she hadn't been distracted by Logan and her own selfish needs, she might have heard someone in the house.

Making love with him had led to the disappearance of her son, and if she had to build a wall in her heart to keep Logan out, she would. Her chest clamped as if caught in a vise. Perhaps Joe had been right—she wasn't fit to be a mother.

As if reading her mind, Logan sought to reassure her. "Stop blaming yourself. This isn't your fault."

Unwilling to face him, she strode into the den. If anything happened to Nicholas, she would never forgive herself. "I should have left, taken him somewhere safe."

Apparently averse to leaving her alone, he followed. "We had no way of knowing someone might return. Even Mike thought it unlikely that the kidnapper would try again."

Why wouldn't he let her be? She stopped pacing and faced him, her voice shaking. "I shouldn't have taken the chance."

Logan winced, and his tone softened. "Stop beating yourself up. You've a home here. Where would you have gone? And who's to say the kidnapper wouldn't have followed?"

Why did he keep badgering her? She couldn't weaken and accept his attempt to console her. Didn't he know she was about to fall apart? Weak, useless, Joe had called her. He'd been so certain she would collapse when her son needed her, but she couldn't help it.

Yes, you can. Think. Every detail might be important. She took a deep breath and pulled herself together. When the police arrived, she had to be coherent.

Within minutes, the patrol car pulled into the drive, and she ran through the chilly garage and outside. Two police officers, one male, one female, exited the car.

Tara sped toward them, Logan close on her heels. "You've got to find him. Can you call the FBI?"

The woman police officer nodded. "They'll be notified soon, ma'am. But unless we have evidence the criminal crossed state lines, the FBI makes its own decision when to take on a case." The officer patted Tara's arm. "By the way, I'm Dillon. Officer Jones and I will do the preliminary investigation."

"Can you hurry?" Tara pleaded. "My son could be taken farther and farther away."

Officer Dillon took her arm. "First, let's get you inside. There's no point in freezing to death."

Tara led them back into the garage and tried to fill the officers in. "This morning the front door was unlocked, but Logan is sure he locked it last night."

Officer Jones pulled a clipboard from under his arm and started taking notes. "Logan is your husband?"

"I'm a friend." Logan came up beside Tara and put his arm over her shoulder, but she sidled away from his touch.

The cop frowned at him. "You spent the night?"

"Yes." Logan handed Jones his business card.

After noting Logan's full name and address in his report, the officer tucked the card in his front pocket. "Was anyone else here last night?"

Tara wrung her hands. "No."

"Any sign of a break-in?"

"No."

While the man filled in his report, Officer Dillon took over the questions. "Who has access?"

"No one," Logan said. "I just changed the locks."

As they walked through the garage, Ruthie and Marge bore down on them like twin heat-seeking torpedoes.

"What's wrong?" Ruthie asked

"Yeah." Marge echoed, "What happened?"

Jones looked up from his report, and his gaze raked both women. "Are you ladies neighbors?"

"Yes." Tara turned toward her new acquaintances. "Did either of you see anything unusual last night?"

"Ma'am, I'll ask the questions, please," Jones rebuked her. "Did you ladies see anything out of the ordinary? A strange vehicle? Anyone suspicious?"

Marge shrugged. "I woke a little while ago and saw you drive up."

"Nicholas is gone," Tara explained.

Marge and Ruthie gasped in tandem.

Ruthie's eyes filled with tears. "Poor little guy. Is there anything we can do?"

"Ladies, you'll have to stay outside until we investigate the crime scene," said Officer Jones. "Perhaps you could check with some of the other neighbors."

Marge and Ruthie headed outside. Tara, Logan and the officers entered the kitchen single file and gathered around the table. Logan made coffee. Tara paced.

Dillon clicked his pen over his pad. "Is anything else missing?

"No." Logan said.

"Yes." Tara contradicted him. "Nicholas's favorite green dinosaur is gone, the one without a left eye."

Officer Jones gave her a skeptical look. "You're sure?"

"Yes," she said, trying to make her voice stronger. "He had it when he went to bed."

Jones wrote down the missing dinosaur. "Would you mind if we do a thorough search of the house?"

They should be looking outside, not in the house. Tara raised her voice even more. "He's not here."

The female officer gave Tara's shoulder a sympathetic pat. "All the same, let's look one more time."

Logan set down his coffee cup. "I'll search the garage." The world had shifted crazily on its axis, perhaps skewing his perceptions, but Tara's rebuff had shaken him.

He knew she was a wreck, had every right to be. He was shaken, too. But in an emergency, weren't lovers supposed to stick together? Her refusal to share her anguish, and her rejection of his touch, hurt more than he'd thought possible.

Perhaps he was being overly sensitive. She wasn't thinking clearly, either. But she obviously didn't want him around, so maybe the best thing would be to give her breathing room.

In the garage, Marge appeared as if she'd been waiting for him. Why wasn't she out searching the neighborhood? He considered asking aloud, then decided not to let the woman waste his time.

Striding to the far corner where some extra plywood left over from Barbara's renovations was stacked, he tilted the panels back to reveal boxes of tile and extra grout, Formica and an empty fluorescent light box. No baby.

Marge peered around him, standing so close her breast brushed his back. He turned, and she boldly rubbed against him. It was uncanny how her features resembled Tara's, and yet where he found Tara's straight nose appealing, this woman reminded him of a witch.

Red-taloned fingernails clutched his arm. "Do you think we're in danger?"

"From what?" He jerked away from her and her cloying perfume. She wasn't making sense.

She followed him to a pile of concrete blocks stacked too tight for a child to crawl between. "I'm scared."

"Spare me the dramatics."

Marge threw herself against his chest with a sob. "You don't know what it's like to lose a child."

"And you do?" Logan removed her arms from around him and stepped toward the kitchen. Was the woman nuts? Or just lonely, pregnant and scared?

When he gently pushed her back, a tremor wracked her. "Don't be like this."

He didn't have time for this. Not now when Nicholas was missing and every precious second counted. Logan whirled around, hands planted on hips, and towered over her. His tone brooked no refusal. "Don't be like what?"

Tears brimmed in Marge's eyes. The dark shadows under her eyes stood out in her ashen face. "Hard. Cold, like my husband."

"I suggest you go back to him."

"I can't. He left me for another woman."

He might be callous, but Marge wasn't his problem. One distraught woman, one who'd come to mean more than any other woman, was enough for him right now. "I'm sorry, but I really can't help you. Maybe you should get professional help."

At his suggestion, Marge kicked a paint can onto its side. He ignored her childish tantrum. He had to find Nicholas. He turned his back and walked into the house, locking the garage door behind him. Tara had enough troubles of her own. She didn't need Marge's, too.

He found Tara dusting off her hands and climbing to her feet by her bed. One glance at her miserable expression told him they hadn't found Nicholas. His heart ached for her. He'd never felt so helpless in his entire life.

Opening her walk-in closet, he flipped on the light. Boxes lined the back wall. Tara's limited wardrobe hung toward the front, her three pairs of shoes neatly arranged underneath, hats, scarves and gloves piled on a high shelf.

Tara's voice cracked. "I already—"

"Quiet!"

Seconds ticked away while he listened for another scraping noise. Nothing. "I thought I heard something."

"Nicholas!" she shouted.

"Mama?" The muffled word came from the back of the closet.

He started tossing boxes aside. Tara yanked them further out of the closet to give him more room to work.

"Mama's coming, Nicholas. We'll have you out of there in no time."

He carefully set aside a suitcase in the back. After moving another box, Logan could see Nicholas's head, then his chest. "I see him. Easy pal, I'm almost there. Tara, he's fine, but there's a note pinned to his chest. Call Officer Dillon."

"I'm here," the female cop replied.

Tara pushed her way past Logan. "Nicholas."

The baby had grabbed a shoe rack and pulled himself upright with a grin. "Mama?"

Scooping him up, Tara rocked him in her arms. Her voice sounded hoarse with happiness. "Oh, Nicky. Are you okay?"

"Okay. Eat."

Tara wiped away her tears and laughed. While she held her baby, Logan got his first clear look at him. None the worse for his ordeal, Nicholas threw his chubby arms around Tara's neck and gave her a sloppy kiss. Logan placed an arm over her shoulder, and this time, when Tara grinned at him, her relief sent a warm jolt of pleasure through him.

The moment was perfect, except the piece of paper pinned to Nicholas's chest crinkled. He glanced down at letters cut from newsprint that were glued to the paper on Nicholas's chest. Logan read the note aloud. "If you don't take care of me, I'm leaving."

Tara gasped, and Logan felt her trembling beneath his arm and pulled her against him to lend support.

"Who is doing this to us?" she cried.

"Can you remove his pajamas without touching the message?" Dillon asked Tara. "If there're prints, we don't want to smudge them."

"I'll try."

She carried Nicholas into his bedroom and placed him on his changing table. "Has anyone seen his dinosaur? If he's distracted, he won't squirm so much."

"The dinosaur isn't here," Logan replied,

Officer Jones carefully stuffed the pajamas with the message into a plastic bag. "It's a shame they didn't use tape."

"Why?" Logan asked.

"Tape leaves prints. Those pins aren't going to give us much to go on."

"What about the paper?"

"We'll send it to the lab." But Logan could tell from his tone that the officer wasn't hopeful.

"Do you mind if I use your phone?" Dillon asked. "I want to report to Detective Scott."

"In the kitchen," Logan answered. Tara was too busy hugging Nicholas to reply. Now that she could touch him, she couldn't seem to get enough of him.

Logan stepped closer, drawn to mother and baby, both giggling and playing. "Hi, pal. Don't you ever scare your mom like that again."

Nicholas pointed at Logan. "Dadadada."

A startled look entered Tara's eyes. "Where could he have gotten that from?"

Logan chuckled. "I'm afraid I'm responsible."

She picked up Nicholas and held him protectively to her breast. "You taught him to call you dada?"

"Umm, not exactly. I read him the story of the three bears. You know, mama bear, baby bear and daddy bear, and he just sort of assumed . . ."

"Eat. Eat. Eat."

Logan and Tara exchanged smiles over Nicholas's head. The world was suddenly back the way it was supposed to be. But from the edge of his vision, Logan saw the plastic bag dangling from the officer's fingers. They might have Nicholas safely back, but they could no longer deny someone was after him.

They entered the kitchen, and Officer Dillon held out the phone to Logan. "Mike wants to talk to you."

Logan took the receiver. "What's up?"

"When the first kidnap attempt on Nicholas occurred, Conrad Pemberton was having dinner with a senator."

Logan sighed. "Thanks, Mike." He repeated the message to the others, hoping the police would solve this case soon.

"This whole thing is very strange," Dillon said.

Logan hung up the phone with a frown. "If someone's after Nicholas, why didn't they take him when they had the chance? Why the note?"

"Because—" Tara paused to wipe off Nicholas's sticky hands "—my father-in-law intends to take Nicholas away from me in court."

"What do you mean?" Jones asked.

"To get legal custody of Nicholas, Conrad must show I'm unfit. What better way to prove that than by police records of a woman who can't keep track of her child . . ."

". . . While she slept in front of the fire with her boyfriend?" A light of understanding lit Officer Jones's eyes.

"Exactly."

"But Mike just said Conrad was having dinner with a senator the first time someone tried to take Nicholas," Logan argued.

Tara set Nicholas on the floor. "And he'll have just as good an alibi this time. He probably hires people to do his dirty work."

The baby crawled over to Logan, and he picked him up. "The first time, someone actually tried to *take* Nicholas. This time, they only played games. Why the change?"

In the silence, Jones put away his clipboard. "Only a sick mind would do this."

Nicholas patted Logan's shoulder. "Dadada."

"Lo-gan." Logan said his name slowly, but the kid paid no attention.

After the police left, Tara and Logan settled in the den. Nicholas played with his toys, and Logan took a chair across from Tara on the couch.

Leaning forward, he rested his arms on his knees. "Why don't you come and stay at my house?"

She fidgeted with a corner of an afghan. "I couldn't ask you to put us up."

"You're not asking. I'm offering. Besides, you can't stay here. It's not safe. Before, we thought the kidnapping was a one-time hit and run. Now we know better."

Tara gazed at Nicholas contentedly playing with his plastic blocks. Her son threw Logan a block, and to Nicholas's delight, he caught it and tossed it back.

Already, Nicholas treated Logan like a family member. And what about her? Was she coming to depend on Logan too much? The idea made her numb. But what did that matter compared to Nicholas's safety? She had no job, very little money and nowhere else to go.

"We won't be in your way?"

"It'll be a relief to have you. I'll be able to concentrate on getting a bid out instead of worrying about you." Logan stood and wandered to the fireplace. "Go pack a few things, and I'll watch Nicholas."

Tara gathered the essentials and carried everything to the front door. Logan loaded his truck. "Babies certainly come with a lot of paraphernalia."

Tara grinned. "He needs the car seat, a playpen and a high chair is a good idea, too."

"Have we got enough baby food for a few days?"

When had Logan started saying *we* instead of *you?* Sometime during last night, their relationship had changed, and he'd obviously begun to think of them as a couple. The thought made her squirm on the front seat of the truck. Although it felt good to have a wonderful man care enough about her and her son to offer his home to them, she had to dwell on more practical matters. Right now, her thoughts had to stay firmly on Nicholas and finding another job, but how could she look for work if she was forced into hiding?

Leaning over the steering wheel, Logan placed the car seat between them. While he secured the seat, she snapped Nicholas in tight.

They pulled out of the subdivision, and the sun slipped behind a cloud. Logan reached up, adjusted the rearview mirror and flipped on the radio. Nicholas started kicking his feet to the sound of an old Beatles tune.

Tara fastened her seat belt. "How long do you think we'll have to hide?"

"You're welcome to stay until you feel safe again."

Tara squeezed his hand, hoping he wouldn't notice the tears in her eyes. "Thank you."

She'd never be able to thank him enough for all he'd done, but she couldn't let him believe her lapse last night would happen again.

Then, what was last night?

A mistake she wouldn't repeat. Although resisting his charm would be difficult, her first concern had to be Nicholas's safety. She wouldn't stay with Logan long—just long enough to come up with a plan.

Then a new concern worried her. "Is the house in your name?"

Logan glanced into the rearview mirror and frowned. "Yes. Why?"

"Because Conrad knows your name. He'll find us."

Again his eyes flicked to the mirror. "I think someone is following us."

Tara started to turn around to look. "Sit still," he ordered. "I don't want to alert them that we've noticed."

Without increasing his speed, Logan took a right, another right, and then a left. In a side mirror, she watched a green Oldsmobile follow their every turn.

Her pulse shot up. "What should we do?"

"After all of our turns, it wouldn't take a rocket scientist to figure out we know they're tailing us."

"The car just speeded up."

Several loud retorts, like a car backfiring, sounded close by.

"Get down. They're shooting at us!" Logan stepped on the gas and swung the vehicle around a sharp curve.

Her heart skittered. Her hand flew to the baby seat.

Chapter Ten

Tara has everything that should be mine. Damn her. But soon the walls would close in around her, until she'd have nowhere else to run, or hide. Without a college education, without family connections, she'd never amount to anything but a futile, pathetic flop.

The first part of the plan had worked with brilliant efficiency. Tara no longer had a job and must be almost out of money. And she no longer had a safe haven to call home.

Soon she wouldn't have a friend, either. Logan Stone did not belong with her. Just as Tara had lost her job and home, she'd lose him, too.

Tara would be left, cornered and cowering, with only her baby. And then, the child, too, would be ripped from her, until she had nothing. Nothing.

A shaking hand jerked in surprise at the sudden footstep. Lips white with tension released a gasp. "Where have you been?"

"In Switzerland, on business. Their banks have the best reputation for privacy." He plucked the toy dinosaur off the chair, a look of weary anticipation on his face. "Where's Nicholas?"

"When you didn't return on time, I changed the plan."

He heaved the dinosaur onto the floor and folded his arms across his chest. "You better have a good reason for the delay. I can't afford to be seen."

"Oh, I have very good reasons. I want her to suffer. I want fear to become her best friend, invade her dreams, take over her soul."

He sighed and set down his briefcase on a dusty coffee table. "What's the point? She's going to lose her son. Isn't that enough?"

"But if the loss came as a surprise, there would be nothing she could do. This way, she'll suffer because she had fair warning."

"Making her suffer was never part of this. You're twisting my plan for some ridiculous concept of revenge. Isn't the money and the child enough for you?"

"I want more."

His eyes narrowed with icy fury. "What else is there?"

"Satisfaction for the years I waited while she took what was mine without thought of the consequences."

"Have you lost your mind? How dare you alter the schedule? Any delay places us at risk of capture. Even now, we don't know if she'll return to Barbara's house."

"It doesn't matter. Wherever she goes, I will find her. I know how she thinks. I know where she is. She cannot hide from me."

TARA TWISTED AROUND in the car for a quick look behind her. She saw little traffic. A few pedestrians walked along the street, and shopkeepers cleared their sidewalks of snow. When Logan took a sharp left around the two-story bank, the green Oldsmobile followed them, sliding sideways.

She peered at the driver, but couldn't make out any identifying characteristics. All she could see was a gloved hand holding a gun through the slightly opened tinted window. "Where are we going?"

"Straight to the police station."

More shots came from the driver. Wild shots that had yet to hit their truck.

They slid around a corner. The seat belt dug into her stomach and chafed her neck. The pickup hit a bump and the contents of the diaper bag scattered on the floorboards.

Logan braked, and her stomach flip-flopped. "You aren't thinking of stopping?" she asked.

"Not with them shooting at us. But don't worry too much. Those shots seem really wild—almost as if someone just wants to scare us."

"They're doing a good job," Tara said through gritted teeth.

"I'll try and lose them. Is Nicholas still strapped in tight?"

"Yes."

"Okay. Hold on. Close your eyes if you have to, but don't scream, I need to concentrate."

Logan pressed the gas pedal to the floor, and the truck surged forward. He whipped around a van, and its driver gave them the finger.

A light turned yellow up ahead, and Logan's voice sounded as if it came from far away. "We're going to slide around the bend. It's scary, but a piece of cake. Trust me.''

She gripped the baby's car seat with one hand, clutched the door with the other and braced her feet on the dash. Logan was a stunt driver. He knew what he was doing.

Store lights and a gas station flew by in a blur. Nicholas started to cry. Remembering Logan's need for concentration, she hummed a lullaby to calm Nicholas. Billboards whizzed past in a blur, while her heart did crazy somersaults in her chest.

She risked another glance behind them. Although the green Olds still chased them, it had fallen farther behind. If they didn't crash, they might have a chance of eluding their pursuer.

She hadn't counted on a city bus stranded at curbside. Luckily, the bus appeared vacant, but it was blocking the road.

A shot pinged from somewhere behind them.

Logan swerved right, and the rear of the truck fishtailed into a bank of plowed snow. The truck rose onto two tires, almost on its side, skidding down the road. She closed her eyes, sure they would roll.

But all four tires hit the ground with a thud, and she dared open her eyes. Through a miracle of timing, luck and skill, he'd managed to avoid the bus.

Behind them, the Olds sideswiped the bus and slid toward a newsstand. People scattered, papers flew into the air, and a police siren blared in the distance.

Logan swore, then eased out of the skid, never slowing.

Clear of town, they had to pass through one more light and make a hard right turn before reaching the police station. Logan timed the light perfectly, and they made it through on the green.

A loud clanging around the curve ahead warned of an oncoming train. She'd forgotten the track that ran perpendicular to their road. She estimated they would reach the crossing before the oncoming train, but they were going too fast to stop or turn in front of the speeding engine.

A quick glance in the rearview mirror showed the Olds was still pursuing them, but Logan's driving had gained them a few precious seconds.

He stepped on the gas. "I'll lose them up here."

She peeked out the side window at the track cutting across the road and gasped. He meant to cross the tracks in front of the speeding train, but at their speed, there was no way he could turn. And if they slowed, they'd be shot.

She risked another peek at the Olds, but the car's dark tinted windows prevented her from making out the driver. If only she could see the plates.

At full speed, Logan jammed his foot on the brakes and simultaneously twisted the steering wheel hard away from the tracks, turning them into a two-hundred-and-seventy-degree rotation that left them facing the railroad crossing. For a moment during their dizzying spin, she lost her view of the Olds, and then it briefly came into view. Her gaze dropped to the plates, and she memorized the first four digits before it spun out of her line of sight.

The train whistle blared a warning. Nicholas screamed, and Tara held her breath. Could they make it? Ignoring everything, Logan sped between the barriers just ahead of the speeding train.

They'd made it. Logan had kept them safe.

The Olds had failed to anticipate Logan's maneuver. The car had ended facing the wrong direction with no time to follow.

Logan's voice was calm. "We lost them."

Tara swallowed. "I think I'm going to be sick."

"Try not to think about it. I don't want to stop until we reach the police station."

But he slowed, and opened her window. The icy air slapped her reeling senses back to normal, and she drew deep, fortifying breaths.

After closing the window, she turned to Nicholas. He'd stopped crying, but his face was still red and wet. "Mama's here, baby."

"Don't take him out of the car seat yet," Logan warned.

"The way you drive, I wouldn't think of it."

"I did the best I could." Tara saw the ghost of a grin play around his mouth. "I think we're safe now, but check the side mirror periodically."

She drew a deep breath and let it out. "I suppose you're used to that kind of speed, but I was scared to death."

His gaze darted right, left, to the rearview mirror. "No one is used to driving like that. Stunt work isn't like the chase scenes you see in the movies. We choreograph each practice run. And the cars and trucks have special equipment to protect stunt people."

She raised a brow, her pulse finally slowing. "You mean the fact we escaped in one piece was pure luck?"

This time the grin erupted. "I'd like to think I had something to do with it. Remember that last turn?"

She shuddered, recalling the sick feeling as they twirled and her stomach lurched. "I'll never forget it."

"If I'd turned a quarter turn instead of three quarters, they would have guessed my intentions. When they finally realized which way I was headed, they couldn't react quickly enough to get by the train."

Once again she owed him big time. "How can I thank you for saving our lives?"

He shot her a mocking leer and spoke with a fake Hungarian accent. "You could warm my bed, pretty woman."

His attempt to lighten her mood worked, and she gained confidence with every mile driven without a sign of their pursuer. She straightened in her seat and handed Nicholas a toy. "I saw the first four digits of the license plate."

"Great." He flashed her a look of admiration. "Mike will find the car's owner in no time. Let's hope the vehicle's not stolen."

Logan had been overly optimistic. The police computer system was down due to the storm, and no one knew when the lines would be working. A day or two at most, Mike promised.

So after giving their report, they were once again on their way to Logan's cabin in the mountains. He negotiated steep, winding roads cleared of snow. The only signs of civilization were mailboxes along the road and chimney smoke from houses hidden in the woods.

While the mountains might make an ideal place to stay temporarily, she and Nicholas couldn't keep running. Tara had watched enough football games with

Joe to remember the best defense was often a strong offense.

By the time Logan pulled into his unplowed drive, she had come up with an idea, but didn't mention it to him immediately. Instead, she took in the picturesque setting. A log cabin built in an A-frame shape perched in a clearing on the side of the mountain. Huge windows overlooked the surrounding woods without a neighbor in sight to spoil the view. Even if the kidnapper found Logan's address, no one could make it up this long, winding drive without detection.

A humongous German shepherd bounded out a swing door in the garage and barked a greeting. Logan grinned and tousled the dog's fur. "Miss me?"

"You've been gone for a while. He must be starving," Tara said, hating to think of the magnificent animal's suffering on her account.

When he stepped out of the truck, the huge dog leapt up on his hind legs, put his paws on Logan's chest and tried to lick his face. "Mrs. Phillips, a next-door neighbor, brings me fresh eggs every morning and cleans once a week. When I'm gone, she feeds Ace and looks after my place. Ace's starved for attention, not food."

"Dog. Dog. Dog." Nicholas bounced in Tara's arms and stretched toward the huge animal.

"Does he like children?" she asked, trying not to think about how many other nights Logan hadn't come home.

"Down, boy," Logan commanded. With tail wagging, Ace walked over to her. "He's terrific with kids, and he's a great watchdog. Let him sniff both of you."

Nicholas wriggled, his hand outstretched toward the dog. "Dog." Ace licked his hand, and he laughed.

She carried Nicholas up an unshoveled path with Logan gripping her elbow to steady her. After unlocking the door, he stepped back to let her enter first.

Polished hardwood floors, broken up by area carpets and burgundy leather furniture, greeted her gaze. Potted ferns decorated a reading corner where magazines and books lay scattered across a coffee table. A massive stone fireplace dominated the cozy room. Lighting from the two-story ceiling spotlighted Logan's train collection which lined wooden cabinets along one pine wall.

When she could tear her gaze from the luxurious room to Logan, she caught him watching her with a look of amusement on his face. "Surprised?"

She had imagined a bare little cabin in the words, not a comfortable sanctuary from the world. And she hadn't expected to feel immediately at home, either. "I never thought of you as settled."

"Oh?"

"I just assumed you were waiting for your knee to heel so you could return to Hollywood and stunt work."

"I'm never going back." He limped over to the huge fireplace, its giant logs already laid in the grate. With one sure flick of the wrist, he brushed the match against the gray stone and he lit it, much in the way his hands stroked her flesh, lighting her on fire with a simple caress. Within minutes the fire crackled merrily.

"Down." Nicholas demanded, apparently eager to explore.

"It's okay." Logan knelt beside the fire and scratched Ace behind his ears. "My sisters' kids come to visit often, so the pesticides are locked up, the cabinets have safety locks, and the fireplace is too tall for him to crawl into."

"What about breakables?"

"Out of his reach."

Nicholas wriggled to the floor and made a beeline for Ace.

LATER THAT AFTERNOON, they carried in her luggage and the baby paraphernalia. Then, after they had eaten, Nicholas lay asleep on the floor next to Ace, his head pillowed on the dog's stomach. Logan's home easily absorbed them, the crib fitting neatly into a corner of the den and Nicholas's high chair beside the kitchen table.

With dog and baby settled, Logan took Tara on a tour of his home. She noted with surprise crayoned pictures, drawn by his nieces and nephews, stuck to the refrigerator with magnets. Amish quilts covered the queen-size bed in the guest room. His office, the only messy room in the house, had a copy machine, a fax and what looked like the latest in computer hardware. Signed pictures of Logan standing alongside smiling celebrities hung on the wall.

"I built this place with savings from the stunt business. Now I'm working to maintain my life-style by bidding on that construction job." He gestured to a stack of blueprints covering his desk.

One glance at the wall space over his desk, and she knew it was reserved for family. For one moment, she imagined a picture of herself holding Nicholas with

Logan's arm over her shoulder in the middle of the others, a permanent feature. Then she banished the thought, knowing this could only be a temporary haven until she set her life in order.

Her gaze focused on the pictures of his sisters and mother, noting they all had the same dark, unmistakably sexy eyes as Logan. But there was just one picture of his father, a tall, distinguished-looking man in his mid-thirties.

"He died when I was thirteen."

No wonder Logan was so protective. He'd become the man of his house at an early age, and from the sound of his voice, he still mourned the loss of his father. She knew what it was like to lose people she loved and yearned for children to make up for the loneliness of her childhood.

"Do you remember your dad?" She couldn't keep the wistfulness from her voice.

"Of course." He turned from the blueprints on his desk to meet her gaze. "You've never told me about your family."

She shrugged and let out a long breath. "There isn't much to tell. My parents died in a plane crash when I was two. An elderly great-aunt looked after me, then she died of cancer when I was six. After that I lived in foster homes."

He reached out and gave her hand a gentle squeeze. "I'm sorry." The sound of his husky voice rippled down her spine like a caress.

"I've never had a home of my own. After I married, the house Joe and I lived in...well, it was *his* house. When I moved in, it was fully furnished, and if I so much as turned a chair in a different direction, Joe corrected my error.''

He hesitated as if suddenly wary of probing her past. "You two seem so mismatched. How did you meet?''

Did he think her so fragile she couldn't speak about the past without shattering into pieces? Annoyed with herself for giving him that impression, she spoke firmly. "I was working at a video store to put myself through college, and he walked in to rent a movie.''

Explaining was more difficult than she'd thought, and while she hadn't realized that until she'd tried to put her story into words, somehow he had sensed her pain. His sympathetic gaze when she caught him watching her fiddle with the paperweight on his desk made her continue. Better to get the story out so it would no longer be a barrier between them. "The first time we met, Joe must have stared at me for an hour without saying one word. Later he told me he'd been tongue-tied because he found me so beautiful. At the time, I believed him. Now, I'm not so sure.''

Logan leaned against his desk, his back to the window, and the bright afternoon sunlight cast his face in shadow. "Why?''

She stared past him, through the window. Despite the cold outside, the loss of her job, the threat to her son and her uncertain future, she was glad to be here with him and share her thoughts. As she let out the words that she'd kept to herself for so long, it felt like a great weight lifted from her heart.

"I wasn't from his social class, couldn't equal his Ivy League educational background. Wasn't even the same religion. He told me that didn't matter and I believed him. But the day I married him, he became another person." She hesitated. "I think he had ulterior motives."

"What do you mean?" Logan asked softly.

She didn't reply but lowered her eyes. He came around his desk, cupped her chin in his callused palm and lifted her gaze to meet his.

It wasn't easy telling him about another man, not when she so badly wanted to forget how she'd let Joe take advantage of her, but she wanted Logan to understand. "I think he liked the fact that I had no family. He chased away the few friends I did have, all except Barbara." Tara let out a shaky chuckle. "She called me at work."

Logan's fingers frolicked down her neck, and she leaned into him, breathing in his masculine essence mixed with the scent of smoke and leather. "It seemed like he wanted to isolate you. Maybe he loved you so much he couldn't stand to share you with anyone else."

The possessive look in Logan's eyes made her heart pound. He was attributing Joe with qualities her first husband never possessed.

"Joe often said he never wanted anyone else's opinions to come between us." She snuggled against his chest, feeling safe, warm and protected. "Of course, early on, I knew something was wrong in our marriage. At first I thought it was me. I never pleased him, no matter how hard I tried. Eventually, I stopped trying, and Nicholas became the focal point of my existence. He was the only person in the world who loved me, and I would do anything for him."

"Did Joe threaten him?" His harsh tone hinted about what he thought of someone hurting her son. Logan couldn't have been more protective of Nicholas if he'd been his own child.

"On the contrary, Joe was too watchful. He read baby nutrition books, even weighed the food before Nicholas swallowed it. He made him listen to classical music for hours. Every piece of furniture had name tags, so our son would learn to read."

Logan pulled back and stared at her, his brow creased in a frown. "But Nicholas is just a baby."

"Joe said it was imperative that Nicholas learn to read by age three so he would be accepted to the best preschool and later the top private schools. And if he didn't go to the finest prep school, he'd never be admitted to Princeton. Pembertons go to Princeton."

"Unbelievable." He peered at her with concern. "So he had the kid's whole life mapped out, and you were caught in the middle."

Although she'd known deep in her soul that Joe had been wrong, it comforted her to hear Logan agree with her. She drank in his understanding gaze the same way parched desert sand soaks up a long-awaited rain. "I was afraid Nicholas would grow up warped. The day before Joe died, we had a huge fight." She rubbed her arms as if to ward off the frosty memories.

"We don't have to talk about this if it makes you sad." He put his hands over hers but nothing warmed her, not even his attempt to let her leave the past behind.

She wanted to explain. Maybe the confession would cleanse her and she could finally put the past behind. And yet her memories of Joe were cold and ugly. A shiver crawled down her spine, and she lowered her voice. "I heard Joe talking on the phone about money. Lots of money. I suspected Conrad was on the other line, although I don't know that for sure."

"What did Pemberton think of your marriage?"

Sensing his perusal of her, she gave him a sideways glance, then made a lame attempt to pretend her father-in-law's rejection didn't matter. When her gaze met his approving one and she discovered pure male sympathy, she was encouraged to tell him the rest. "Conrad was furious when Joe first told him we would marry. He threatened to disinherit Joe."

"Did he?"

She rubbed her palms on her thighs. "I don't know. Joe went over one Saturday and had a long talk with his father. When he returned, he said he'd patched things up. After that, I was accepted, if not warmly welcomed, into my father-in-law's home. When I became pregnant, Conrad was so delighted I thought everything might finally work out."

"Unfeeling people usually act that way to everyone. It seems odd that Joe would show so much caring for his son and none for you." Logan sighed and shot her a speculative look. "Maybe Joe couldn't inherit the family trust fund until he produced an heir?"

She hadn't thought of that. How different it was, sharing her thoughts with Logan, sharing his warmth, than it had been to face Joe and his odd coldness alone. "The moment Joe realized I was listening to his conversation, he hung up the phone." Tara shrugged. "If there was a trust fund, Joe never mentioned it to me. But his family's money was not that important."

"You don't want diamonds and furs?" Logan teased.

"I'd settle for paying my bills." She turned and placed her hands on his shoulders. "I've lost so many people in my life, I can't lose Nicholas, too. He's all I have. I couldn't bear it if something happened to him." She didn't want to lose Logan, either. His solid feel, his scent, his arms around her, seemed a safe haven. He gave her an inner security she'd never felt before. She twisted her hands in his sweater, stared down at his blueprints, eyes bleary. "This morning when we couldn't find Nicholas, I panicked. If I withdrew from you . . . well, I couldn't help myself."

"I understand," he said softly, claiming her lips. She greeted his mouth with an eager mixture of anticipation and excitement, pleased he still wanted her after what she'd divulged. There was a dreamy intimacy to their kiss, one of understanding and burning sweetness. She could learn so much about sharing and caring from this man, but first she wanted to give herself to him wholeheartedly and without reserve.

But she couldn't make love knowing someone wanted to kidnap her son. Until Nicholas was free of danger, she had to concentrate on keeping him safe.

Reluctantly, she pulled away from Logan's arms. "I should check Nicholas."

Without a word of rebuke, Logan closed his blueprints and they walked arm in arm back to the great room.

Nicholas hadn't moved from his position by the German shepherd, and Tara settled on a leather sofa and pulled a black, white and gray Amish quilt across her lap. "We can't wait for something else to happen. We've got to go on the attack."

"I'm sure Mike is doing the best he can." Logan went to the kitchen area and returned, handing her a cup of hot chocolate with marshmallows floating on the surface.

She smiled in appreciation. Her husband had never waited on her like that. "But he has other cases to worry about, not just us. Besides, we aren't the police, so we don't have to concern ourselves with legalities."

Logan shook a finger at her. "If you think we can rig a trap and wait for the kidnapper to enter the house, that could send us both to jail."

"I have an idea that will clear my name with Equity Real Estate. I need to make a long-distance phone call." She took a piece of paper from her purse, unfolded the telephone number and dialed.

"Rutherford Everhart residence."

"Mr. Everhart, please."

She gripped the phone tight while the butler called her first real-estate client, the man she'd supposedly propositioned, to the phone. Logan sat beside her with a gleam of approval in his warm gaze.

"Hello?"

"Mr. Everhart, I'm Ms. Simpson from Donaldson, Dailey and Fry, an investigative firm in Harden, New Jersey, hired by Equity Real Estate. We want to make absolutely sure that the woman who propositioned you is Tara Larson. If you saw her picture, could you identify this woman?"

At her lie, Logan's jaw dropped. But as she continued the conversation, he caught on to her tactic, and
his lips widened into a grin.

"Yes. I already told Mr. Bittner. The woman was
blond, thin, about five foot seven."

"And she attacked you?"

"She came right up to me and grabbed my pri-
vates."

If they could meet, he would see she wasn't the same
woman who had accosted him. "Could I fax you her
picture?"

"Well, I suppose so." He gave her his fax number,
and Tara hung up the phone with a satisfied smile. She
took a snapshot, a picture of herself and Nicholas,
from her wallet and handed it to Logan. After blocking out her son's image with paper, they faxed her
likeness.

Five minutes later, Tara called Everhart back. "Did
you get the fax? Is that the same woman who attacked you?"

"I think so."

How could that be possible? The man must be mis-
taken. "You're sure?"

"Well, this picture is tiny, but it sure looks like the
same woman."

She thanked him for his help and slowly hung up the
phone in frustration. She'd been so sure her picture
would clear her, and disappointment washed over her.
"He still claims I accosted him. Do you think he could
be lying so he can sue?"

"It's possible. Or your father-in-law could have set
up the entire incident to get you fired. Maybe he paid

the man to lie. Either way, I'm proud of your initiative."

A warm thrill went through her at his compliment. It felt good to do something positive for a change, and she felt even better that Logan had approved of her idea. And she had another plan to bring the kidnapper into the open, but it required a trip into Harden. "When Nicholas wakes up from his nap, can we drive into town for a little shopping?"

Chapter Eleven

For once, luck was with them. They told Detective
Scott their plan and he agreed to meet them in town at
three. While they killed an hour waiting for him, Tara,
Nicholas and Logan drove into town, stopped at a
Wal-Mart and bought the necessary items to carry out
their plan.

Most of the evidence of their terrifying drive
through town had been cleaned up. The newsstand was
back in business, albeit with a heavy canvas tarp in
place of a wooden roof.

Harden was typical small-town Jersey. Main Street
boasted a theater, styling salon, drugstore and several
boutiques. Pedestrians hurried along the shoveled
walks on errands, waving to neighbors and occasionally stopping to gossip. Tara kept looking over her
shoulder in an attempt to catch sight of the green Olds,
but never spotted it.

They entered a toy store, and Nicholas broke into an
excited grin at the battery-operated dog doing back
flips next to the entrance. Logan plucked an identical
boxed toy from the shelf and propped it under his
arm. "It's time I bought him another present."

Tara shook her head but softened her words with a smile. "You'll spoil him."

"Ball." Nicholas grabbed a paddle with a ball attached to it by a long rubber band.

"No." She twisted the toy gently from her son's grasp and replaced it on the shelf.

Logan laughed. "I haven't been in here in years, but it still smells the same. The boys' stuff is to the right, the girls' to the left."

A salesclerk materialized in front of them. "Can I help you find something?"

"We're looking for a doll," Tara said. "Baby-sized and lifelike."

"Aisle three."

After making their selection, they returned to Logan's truck, ahead of schedule. Into the front seat, Tara placed the most lifelike doll she'd ever seen, along with the dog Logan had insisted on buying for Nicholas.

Logan arranged their purchases next to the items they'd bought at Wal-Mart, covered them with a tarp and glanced at his watch. "We still have half an hour until Mike gets off from work. How about an ice cream?"

In this weather? He must have an internal thermostat set on super high. She remembered the warmth of him when they'd made love, the feeling of belonging Logan gave her. From the beginning he'd made it clear they were in this together, and that meant so much after spending a good part of her life alone. Although she yearned to daydream of a future with Logan, Nicholas had to be her first priority. "I'll take a hot chocolate."

Logan led her and Nicholas into a café-drugstore that doubled as the general town meeting place. After they'd slipped into a booth and ordered, Marge Henley walked in.

Her nosy neighbor waved, bought a magazine and walked over. "So this is where you ran off to." She glanced at the baby. "I can't believe you're taking Nicholas out in this weather."

"The fresh air will do him good." Tara didn't like the criticism. Properly dressed babies could withstand a little cold air.

"I can only stay a minute." Marge scooted into the booth next to Logan, much closer than necessary. When he lifted a hand to get the waitress's attention, Marge's hand clutched his.

And she didn't let go. "Nothing for me, thanks. I just wanted to let you know I'll be gone for a few days."

Tara and Logan exchanged a long glance over the table. If she read his raised eyebrows correctly, he found Marge's behavior as bizarre as she did.

Logan extracted his hand from Marge's grip. Tara liked the way he never gave her reason to feel jealous. Joe had never made her feel jealous, either. But Logan was different. He made it clear that to him, she was the most important woman, the woman he wanted.

When Logan shifted away, Marge didn't seem to notice. Her face was flushed and excited. "Joseph and I are going to try and patch things up."

"Joseph?" Tara gasped.

"My husband. Isn't it great that he's back?"

Without waiting for an answer, Marge slid out of the booth and hurried on her way. Logan dug into his ice cream. "She tried to put her hand on my thigh. Does that sound like she's anxious to make up with her husband?" His voice indicated his disgust.

"Some women aren't happy unless they have every man in the room panting after them. She's probably a very insecure person."

He cocked a brow. "You're not jealous?"

Tara was about to answer when Detective Scott strode into the café and walked up to their table with a friendly smile. "I got off early. Is everything ready?"

"Yes." Logan wiped his mouth with a napkin and left a tip beside his dish.

Mike didn't stay at their table. He walked past them, said several more hellos and bought a newspaper.

Tara dressed her son, who was surprisingly quiet. He'd been too busy looking at his new surroundings to do more than sit contentedly in her arms and stare.

For the next hour, Tara, Logan and Nicholas showed themselves all over town. They shopped in several boutiques, checked out the video store and wandered through the bookshop.

They met Mr. and Mrs. Phillips on the street beside Logan's truck, just as Nicholas became cranky. Logan had known the older couple for years. They owned the cabin next to Logan's, and Mrs. Phillips often brought him fresh eggs from their chickens.

Despite Logan's confidence in the couple, Tara looked them over carefully but could find nothing to alarm her in Mrs. Phillips's kindly face or Mr. Phillips's worried one. They seemed just what Logan said they were—honest, decent people.

As the four of them stood together on the street, blocking the view of any curious watchers, the heavyset Mrs. Phillips whisked Nicholas protectively under her billowy coat. "I'll take good care of him. Don't you worry none, dear."

Tara clutched the doll Logan thrust into her arms. Was she making a gigantic mistake? Should she leave her son with strangers? The older couple walked away with Nicholas hidden, and her chest tightened.

From a distance, she caught Mike watching the exchange. He gave Tara a slight nod and turned away.

"Come on. Get in." Logan opened her door to his truck, and she climbed in, trying not to let the tears gathering in her eyes spill down her cheeks.

By the time Logan walked around the truck and started the engine, she'd regained a little self-control. Logan smoothed the hair on her brow. "Hey, this was your idea."

"I know." Still, a cold doll was no substitute for a warm, breathing and kicking Nicholas. Her arms ached with a hollow emptiness. "I hate letting my baby out of sight."

"They'll take Nicholas back to their place. After that high-profile trek through town, the kidnapper should be watching *us,* not them."

She sighed, exhausted by the ordeal of wondering if someone had watched their every move. "Do you think this is going to work?"

Logan switched on the radio to an easy-listening station. "There's no harm in trying. Strap the doll into the car seat and don't forget to cover it with the blanket.''

Dressed in an outfit identical to Nicholas's, the doll would fool most casual observers. Logan had rigged a tape recorder of Nicholas's voice to the bottom of the car seat, and the doll said baby words. And if Tara pressed a certain button, the doll moved in incredibly lifelike ways.

They stopped at the grocery store and transferred the car seat, with the doll, its face hidden by Nicholas's blanket, to a grocery cart. Several times, Tara spotted Mike following them, but she followed orders and didn't acknowledge his presence.

Logan headed down the cereal isle, and Tara deliberately left her cart with the doll unattended to stand at the crowded deli counter. No one took the bait.

Disappointed that the kidnapper hadn't made a move toward the vulnerable doll, they checked out a few groceries and returned to the truck. Logan drove for a block and pulled into the parking lot of the hardware store. ''Hey, try and relax. Let's both go inside and leave the bait here.''

She got out of the truck and stomped her cold feet. ''Okay. My nerves can't take much more of this.''

His arm went round her shoulders, and he led her away from the truck toward the front door. ''You're doing fine. Kiss me?''

''Not here,'' she protested.

His dark eyes twinkled with mischief. ''Come on. Pretend Mike's not watching. Make it look like we're so wrapped up in each other, we've forgotten the baby.''

Heat stole up her cheeks. "That's the flimsiest excuse to steal a kiss that I've ever heard."

"Woman, shut up and kiss me!"

Two could play this game. Flinging herself against his chest, she tugged his head down and nibbled on his lips. His heat chased away her fear. Back in his arms, for the moment, she forgot their plan and the passersby. For a moment, only the two of them existed, wrapped together in an eddy of swirling bliss. She'd intended to turn him on and pull away teasingly, teach him not to demand what she wasn't ready to give.

But she hadn't counted on the embers inside her that he'd stoked into a blaze. Her head reeled and her knees melted. When a dark brown UPS truck pulled into the parking lot, neither of them paid much attention. Even though the truck parked between them and Logan's truck, if someone made a move toward the doll, it was Mike's job to catch the kidnapper, not theirs.

When Logan finally pulled away, she had no idea how long the kiss had lasted. She felt like a breathless teenager sparking in the parking lot without a care in the world. Anyone could have watched their kiss. But no one paid the least attention to them. Everyone was focused on an ambulance. Siren wailing, it moved down Main Street followed by several police cars, blue lights flashing.

"Let's see what's going on." Logan took her hand and led her toward the street. About fifty people were congregated around a knot of paramedics.

Mike hurried over to Tara and Logan with a guilty look on his face. "Sorry I didn't hold up my end of the deal. A little girl got hit by a car. I had to stay with her until the experts arrived."

They watched the paramedics strap the little girl onto a stretcher and load her into the ambulance. Her mother climbed into the back of the vehicle and took the child's hand, tears streaming down her face.

Tara spoke past the lump in her throat. "Will she be okay?"

Mike nodded. "They think so. But at her age, it's safer to have a doctor check her out. It's a good thing the fire station is right down the block, or she'd have frozen lying in the snow."

"That's how they got here so fast." Logan turned around and frowned. "What about the doll?"

They rushed to his truck. Tara's heart pounded against her rib cage. At the sight of Logan's door standing wide open, the tiny hairs on her arm stood on end. The car seat with the doll inside was gone.

She slumped against Logan, uncaring that she needed his strength. "They're still after Nicholas. Damn it. They can't have my baby."

His arms wrapped around her and gently rocked. "Shhh. He's safe."

"We don't know that." A sob caught in her throat. "I'll never know that unless I'm holding him."

Mike knelt in the snow and picked up a round object. Made of gold, the cuff link shone dull yellow against the pebbled ice. "Do the initials CBP mean anything to you?"

Tara fought to keep her voice from sounding hysterical. "That's my father-in-law, Conrad Bruce Pemberton."

Logan clapped Mike on the shoulder. "Let's go."

"Where?" Mike asked.

"After Pemberton."

"We don't have probable cause. Even if we can prove this is Pemberton's cufflink, he could have lost it yesterday, last week, or last year."

"But you found his cuff link on top of the snow," Tara protested. "That must mean he dropped it recently."

Mike shook his head. "Not necessarily. Someone passing by could have kicked it. A plow could have cleared the lot and pushed it to the surface."

Logan's tone deepened in anger. "Are you telling us it's a coincidence that Pemberton wants her kid, the doll disappeared, and you just happened to find his cuff link, and it's *not* connected somehow?"

Mike sighed. "What I'm telling you is that, legally, my hands are tied."

They were wasting time. Tara tugged on Logan's arm. "Just because *he* can't snoop around doesn't mean *we* can't. Let's pay my father-in-law a visit."

Mike dropped the cuff link into his pocket. "Check with the neighbors first. Someone might have noticed Pemberton carrying a doll and think it odd enough to remember. I need strong probable cause to obtain a search warrant."

On the way out of town, Tara insisted they stop and call the Phillipses. They assured her Nicholas was fine. Feeling better, she directed Logan to Pemberton's exclusive neighborhood.

"Senator Kellog lives there." Tara pointed out the three-story brick mansion with tall pillars. "Judge Raven, head of New Jersey's Supreme Court, lives in that ranch. Pemberton is the third estate to the left."

Tara gestured toward her father-in-law's immaculate Victorian house. The mansion was settled on the hill like a musty museum and boasted a metal plate on the door to proclaim its registry as a historic building. A curved brick drive, shaded by oaks plucked of their foliage, led to Tiffany stained-glass doors.

"Now what?" Tara asked.

Logan parked in the street. "We need to give Mike a reason to make an arrest or obtain a search warrant. We'll just knock on a few doors and ask if anyone has spotted something out of the ordinary at the Pemberton place."

She snickered. "These people don't answer doors. Their maids or butlers do it for them."

Undeterred, Logan grinned. "Better yet. Servants love to gossip."

"How do you know?"

"I worked at various jobs until my stunt work paid the bills." Logan got out of the truck, walked around the front and opened the door for her with a perfect British accent. "Will there be anything else, madam?"

Logan's silliness dispelled her pessimism. Tara giggled and walked down the street with a lighter step. "Where should we start?"

After combing the area on both sides of the Pemberton house and across the street, Tara's spirits again began to fall. No one had noticed anything unusual like extra deliveries of baby furniture, or Conrad coming and going at odd hours. In this neighborhood, people minded their own business.

She'd just about decided they should give up when the mail truck pulled around the corner. She and Logan shared a long look and, without a word, headed to the next mailbox and waited.

"Have you seen any strangers around the Pemberton place recently?" Logan asked the postal worker.

The man flipped through a stack of mail inside his truck and separated several magazines from a pile. "Don't think so."

"Have you seen any baby stuff, cribs, strollers, that kind of thing?" Tara asked.

The mail carrier rolled a stack of magazines and flicked them into the box. "Now that you mention it, yeah. The other day, Pemberton signed for a registered letter, and I saw a toy dinosaur stuck between two planters in the front hall. I figured one of his grandkids must've left it."

Tara's pulse raced. This was the kind of information they needed. "What color was the dinosaur?" She held her breath.

The mail carrier scratched his head. "Green. That's why the maid must have missed it, hidden in those plants and all."

"Was it missing a left eye?" Tara asked excitedly.

"Got me on that one. I have no idea."

Logan squeezed her hand. "Thank you. You've been very helpful."

They climbed back into the truck and headed for the nearest corner store to call Mike. Again Tara phoned the Phillipses, and she heard her son saying "Eat, eat" in the background.

The nightmare was almost over. Mike would arrest Pemberton, and Nicholas would finally be safe. After all the worry he'd put her through, she wanted to be there, see her father-in-law's face when Mike arrested him. She wanted to see the handcuffs on his wrists.

Until then she couldn't really believe her son was out of danger.

Mike met them in front of Pemberton's stained-glass doors and rang the bell. "We don't have enough evidence for a search warrant. With luck, he'll just invite us in."

Fate was kind. A uniformed maid recognized Tara and invited them into the mahogany-paneled front hall. While the servant went to announce their presence, Logan searched the planter. His hand disappeared between two silk ferns and pulled out a green dinosaur with the left eye missing. "Now you can make your arrest."

The three of them invaded Pemberton's office. Coolly, Conrad dismissed his maid. "What is the meaning of this? How dare you barge into my home!"

"We found this—" Mike held up the dinosaur "—in your front hall. I'm going to take you down to the station for questioning."

Pemberton stood and slapped his palm on his desk. "I have nothing to hide. I'm a law-abiding citizen. I've never seen that stuffed animal before in my life!"

He sounded so outraged, Tara almost believed him. But she knew better.

"You didn't break into your grandson's house," Mike asked sarcastically, "and move him into a closet with a note pinned to his chest?"

"Why would I do that? He's my grandson. I want him safe."

Logan pushed past Mike. "You tried to make Tara look foolish—"

"By hanging around you, she does that all by herself," Pemberton snapped.

Logan raised clenched hands, but Mike stepped between the two men. "That's enough."

Tara's fists rested on her hips, and rage surged through her, giving her courage. "You wanted to make me look like an unfit mother so you could take Nicholas away from me."

Pemberton licked his lips, and he didn't meet her eyes. "I won't deny that I think Nicholas would be better off with me. But I would never do anything to jeopardize his safety."

Mike walked around the desk. "Nicholas's dinosaur disappeared the same day we found your grandson in that closet. Then his toy shows up in your house. How can you explain it?"

Pemberton slumped. "I have many enemies. Someone is setting me up. If I'd committed a crime, I wouldn't be dumb enough to leave evidence in my own home."

"If you have nothing to hide," Mike suggested, "why don't you come down to the station and we'll see if we can clear this up."

"Fine. I'll have my attorney meet us."

Tara didn't feel the satisfaction she thought she would. Although pleased she had stood up to her father-in-law, weariness settled on her shoulders. She didn't watch Mike take Pemberton to his car. Instead she stared out the study window. She wanted to feel happy, but all she felt was relieved.

Logan came up behind her, and his husky tone reverberated in her ear. "It's over. Now you can relax. We'll get the Phillipses to watch Nicholas for a while longer, and I'm going to take you out somewhere special."

WHILE LOGAN SHAMPOOED his hair, he whistled in the shower, eagerly anticipating the evening ahead. He couldn't wait to see how Tara would look all gussied up. They'd stopped by her house to pick up a few things before heading back to his place. She hadn't let him get a glimpse of her dress, but the excitement in her eyes delighted him.

Despite her worry over her son, she'd changed since they met—changed for the better. The haunted look had disappeared from her gaze, laughter came more readily to her lips. Like a butterfly emerging from its cocoon and spreading its wings, Tara was putting the past and her fears behind. In helping her do so, he'd banished his own mistakes to painless memories.

The last few days had been stressful on both of them. He should have completed his bid on the shopping center, but if he worked through the night, he could still turn it in on time. He couldn't have allowed Tara to set her trap alone.

Holding back and letting her call the shots had been difficult, but rewarding. She'd come up with a great plan, and implementing it had kept her busy enough to alleviate her worry. As her self-assurance grew, he'd reaped an unexpected bonus. She'd begun to trust him. Did she have any idea how irresistible he found her confidence?

Stepping out of the shower, he dried himself, wrapped a towel around his waist and walked into his bedroom. A knock sounded on the door.

"Come in," he called out.

Tara entered and grinned. "Aren't you ready yet?"

Logan's jaw dropped, and his mouth went dry. "No wonder you wouldn't let me see that dress!"

He didn't even try not to stare. Off-the-shoulder red sleeves formed a deep V that dipped to reveal the shadow between her breasts. His hands already itched to peel off the dress. He'd never make it to dinner. A sash wound around her midriff from her waist to her slim hips before flaring over incredibly long legs. Hose and heels completed the outfit.

But it wasn't just her clothing that made him want to forget he was a civilized man. In his younger days, he'd had his share of starlets, but none of them had had the gleaming look of love in her eyes that she did. A look that set him afire. As he tamped down the primitive urge to rip the dress off her luscious body, carry her over his shoulder, throw her down on his bed and ravish her until she promised to be his forever, he acknowledged that she affected him like no other woman.

She twirled around, a mischievous grin on her face. "You like it?"

"I like what's in it." He stifled a groan. It had been too long since he had held her, and he closed the distance, intending to take her into his arms.

She must have read the desire in his eyes because she laughed. "Don't you dare take another step closer."

"Huh?"

"If you get this dress wet, I'll never forgive you."

"Whether it gets wet or not is up to you."

Logan paused, watching her reaction. The look on her face was unreadable, but she didn't move. It was way too late to hide how he felt or what he wanted. But after raising three sisters, he shouldn't be surprised that she didn't want her makeup smudged or her dress wrinkled. He couldn't suppress a twinge of disappointment, though.

He turned toward the closet. Behind him, fabric rustled. A zipper unzipped. He turned around in time to see her the dress fall into a heap at her feet.

"If this dress always makes you react like that—" her gaze boldly dipped to the gap in his towel as she stepped out of her heels "—I'll be saving it to use again." She came to him wearing lacy hose, a whisper of silk, and nothing else but a smile.

He sucked in his breath. Three strides closed the distance between them. Her scent wafted up to tease him, and he groaned, then bent his head to kiss her with savage intensity. Her lips parted, and the heady sensation of her yielding mouth urged him on.

Finding the softness of her breasts, his hands caressed her nipples until she squirmed against him, demanding more. Slowly, teasingly, he dipped his hand past her taut stomach and removed the wisp of silk between her legs.

"You feel hot," he murmured, ready to explode.

"On fire," she gasped.

Her arms encircled his neck. He lifted her at the waist, intending to swing her around to the bed. They didn't make it. Forget the comforts of a mattress and sheets. His lady wanted him—now. Her legs wound around his hips, taking him inside her with a rising fury.

He settled them into a chair, which freed his hands to roam over the delectable hollows and valleys of her silky skin. She was so warm, so supple, so delightfully greedy.

She held nothing back, and her eagerness made him want her all the more. His heart took a perilous leap, and there was no looking back.

Moving in a rhythm all her own, she rocked him higher, further, stretching him tight. Passion fluttered its way from his mouth to his groin.

He couldn't last much longer. His mouth captured her breast, sweet, soft, the tip hard. His hand slipped between her thighs and she let out a pleased gasp. Her back arched. Tremors racked her, and he exploded inside her.

Afterward she clung to him so tenderly he never wanted to let her go. Slowly he regained his senses, and the hammering in his heart stilled to a mellow hum. Would he frighten her if he told her he loved her?

"Someday we're going to have to try this in a bed," she murmured in a breathless tone.

How lucky he was to have found her. He kissed her brow, her nose, her cheek. "I—"

The phone beside the bed rang. When she tried to leave him, his arm tightened around her waist. "Don't go."

She drew away. "We should answer the phone. The sitters might be having a problem with Nicholas."

But when she handed him the portable phone, it was Mike's voice that came over the line and chilled him to ice. "An informant close to the kidnapping ring says Pemberton isn't part of it. Besides, your father-in-law had another perfect alibi. I had to release him."

Logan didn't wait to hear more. He broke the connection and dialed the Phillipses' residence. The phone rang. And rang. And rang.

Chapter Twelve

The moment Logan tensed and his brow creased, Tara jumped off his lap. "What's wrong?"

He dropped the phone into the cradle. "Mike released Pemberton."

The cool air on her bare skin sent an icy tremor down her spine. Grabbing a sheet off the bed, she wrapped it around her. *Oh, please, no!* Was Nicholas in danger? She forced words past frozen lips. "When did they let Conrad go?"

"Just now." Logan stepped into his jeans. "We'll get to Nicholas before Pemberton can drive up here. But I just called the Phillipses, and there's no answer."

"Something's wrong." Her chest tightened and blood drained from her face. She couldn't faint. Her baby needed her, and a sense of urgency overwhelmed her.

Logan gave her a quick pat on her shoulder that did nothing to comfort her. "The Phillipses probably just fell asleep in front of the TV."

Nothing he said could reassure her, and she couldn't keep the reproach from her tone. "You told me the Phillipses are night owls. It's only eight."

He donned a shirt and shoved the tail into his jeans. "Maybe they went for a walk. Go get dressed."

Tara threw on slacks, shirt and sweater in record time. They sprinted to the car and she climbed in, gasping for air. She wouldn't breathe easy until Nicholas was once again in her arms.

She'd barely fastened her seat belt when Logan roared down the drive. He broke the speed limit on the way to the Phillipses' house.

As they rounded a sharp bend, she braced her palms on the dash. "Why did Mike free Conrad?"

"Your father-in-law had an alibi. He couldn't have taken the doll because, at the time, he was making a speech in front of two hundred people."

Her temples throbbed. "What about the dinosaur we found in his house?"

"The leather glove, the cuff link, even the dinosaur, aren't probable cause. The glove can't be tied to Conrad, and the cuff link could have been dropped at any time."

Although her father-in-law wouldn't hurt her son, the thought did nothing to ease her fear. Branches, bare and haunting, loomed over the deserted road. The headlights cut through the dark in a blur. Patches of earth showed through the snow, like blood staining a clean white sheet.

Pulling into the driveway with a screech, Logan killed the lights. "Wait here."

She didn't answer or take the time to argue. How could she sit in the truck when her son might be in danger? Shoving open the door, she jumped onto the driveway, her breath puffing clouds of white smoke, and then took off at a run.

On the steep hill, the snow turned to damp ground, muting their footsteps. The moon hid behind a solid shroud of clouds.

Ahead, the Phillipses' house, crouched on the hillside, was completely dark. She sprinted toward the building, and Logan's steps pounded after her. Four strides later, he caught her hand in his, and together they raced up the front steps.

She rang the bell, her heart racing. He banged on the door, making a noise loud enough to frighten the dead. From inside the house, she thought she heard an odd thud.

Grabbing Logan's arm to prevent him from pounding, she put her ear to the door. "Shh. Listen."

A muffled thumping echoed from inside. "Did you hear that?" she whispered.

"Stand back." Logan didn't waste time trying other doors. His good leg kicked a windowpane and broke the glass.

Reaching through the jagged hole, he unlocked the front door. The thumping got louder. They hurried down a dark, broadloomed hallway, and she tripped over the edge of a carpet. He paused to help her up.

"I'm fine," she replied before he asked. She stood and tugged on his hand. "Let's go."

They followed the thumping noise into the den where Logan flicked on the light. Mr. and Mrs. Phillips sat back to back in chairs, a long rope tying them in place. Someone had blindfolded them and taped their mouths. Mrs. Phillips had worked one foot free and was kicking the firewood chest to create the thumping they'd heard.

Tara's gaze darted frantically around the room. "Where's Nicholas?"

Logan removed the blindfold from Mr. Phillips's eyes. The old man winced at the bright light and let out a yelp when Logan removed the tape from his mouth.

"They took him," Phillips said.

"No-o-o-o!" Tara froze. Her hands and feet turned to ice. She couldn't hear, think, feel. Then something inside snapped. "I should never have left my baby." She wailed. Guilt surged throughout her. "They...they took my son." She slumped to the floor, her stomach churned with nausea, and she exhaled in defeat.

"Tara, don't you pass out on me," Logan ordered softly. "Nicholas needs you. Call Mike."

She couldn't move. Couldn't speak. Couldn't even sob. So cold. She didn't think she'd ever be warm again.

The thought of her baby crying out for her lodged a thick lump in her throat. He wouldn't understand what had happened. No one would reassure him with familiar words.

She imagined his eyes swollen from crying, his red face slick with tears of fright, his chubby arms reaching out to an indifferent stranger. Her stomach churned, and heaved dryly. He would grow up thinking she hadn't wanted him, didn't love him—if he grew up.

Logan took in her white face and feared she might keel over. Asking her to call Mike hadn't snapped her out of her stupor, so when he saw that she wasn't going to respond, his hands worked even more furiously on Mr. Phillips's ropes. "Who took Nicholas?"

"Didn't see a thing. They hit me over the head from behind. Next thing I knew, I woke up tied in this chair."

Torn between acquiring information from the old man and comforting Tara, he grimly stuck to the task of freeing Phillips. "You said, *they*. There were two of them?"

"I think so." The old man rubbed his head with a free hand. After Logan had him untied, Phillips removed his wife's gag.

"I didn't see anything, either," Mrs. Phillips added. "But I heard two sets of footsteps before they got me. They didn't say a word."

Finally free to go to Tara, Logan gently lifted her to her feet and held her against his chest. Her hands were cold and she shivered; her entire body trembled.

Clasping her to him while urging her out the door, he shouted orders over his shoulder. "Call the police. Ask for Detective Mike Scott. Tell him we're going to Pemberton's house."

Tara protested dully, but at least she was speaking. "He would never be foolish enough to take Nicholas there."

Wrapping an arm around her waist, he hurried her toward the truck. "Conrad just got out of jail. He couldn't have done this."

"Then, why are we going there?"

"Because someone left that dinosaur in his house. I want a list of every person who's been in and out of his house since Nicholas's toy disappeared."

The moon came out from behind a cloud. She lifted her head questioningly. "You really think we'll find him?"

"Yes."

She'd scared him back there. When he'd searched her face, her expression had been blank, her eyes unfocused. But she seemed to be pulling herself together now, and he reinforced a reason to take action. "I need your help."

"I'll do whatever is necessary to get my son back." Her voice sounded stronger, if a tad brittle.

They drove into Pemberton's exclusive neighborhood to find Mike in front of the old Victorian house. Tara barely waited for the truck to stop before leaping out.

While Logan turned off the engine and walked around his truck to join them, Mike clasped her shoulders to steady her. Under the streetlight, Logan noted Mike's expression and guessed he had news. "What's up?"

"The motor vehicle department finally coughed out a name on the green Olds. The car belonged to a Janice Wilson."

"J-Janice Wilson?" Tara stuttered, a stunned expression on her face.

"You recognize the name?" Mike asked.

Tara's voice registered astonishment. "I never met her, but Janice Wilson was Joe's old girlfriend." She raised her brow. "Why would she want my son?"

"Perhaps Mr. Pemberton has some answers," Mike suggested. "However, he may not want to talk to us."

"He'll talk, whether he wants to or not," Logan muttered.

They walked up the sidewalk toward the house. Tara held Logan's arm tight, thankful he was here with her. Learning independence had been a necessary step, but she'd finally come to the realization that sharing the burden of her agony could get her through this.

Every light seemed to be on. Tara rang the bell, and finally her father-in-law answered the door.

When Conrad recognized them, his eyes narrowed and his jowls quivered. "I have nothing more to say." He started to slam the door.

Logan stuck his foot inside and prevented him from shutting them out.

"Nicholas has been kidnapped," Tara cried out. How could beads of sweat trickle down her forehead when she was so cold? "Please, we need your help to find him."

The old man staggered back. "I don't know anything," he insisted. Nevertheless, he let Logan shove his way into the foyer.

"Janice Wilson has him!" Tara's voice rose an octave. She couldn't help it. She would have slumped to the floor without Logan's support. But she'd get down on her knees and beg if Conrad would give them the information they needed to find her son. "She chased us, fired shots at us, and I'm sure she's the one who took my baby. But why does she want Nicholas?"

Conrad's brow creased. "Janice Wilson?"

"When was the last time you saw Miss Wilson?" Mike asked.

Conrad's face went white. So he knew more than he'd let on, even though his tone remained imperious as ever. "This is going to take a while."

"We don't have a while," Tara protested.

"Come into the study, please," Pemberton instructed.

His gaze refused to meet hers, and Tara knew he was hiding something. She tried to pull herself together, ignore the chills shaking her body. Mike and Logan didn't know Conrad as well as she did, so she clung to Logan, pretending helplessness while watching Conrad from downcast eyes. Her senses leapt with heightened awareness at the thought he knew more than he was willing to admit.

She sat next to Logan on the leather couch in the paneled study. Mike took a wing chair, and Conrad sat behind his massive cherry desk. But Detective Scott didn't let the opulent surroundings stop him from asking hard questions. "When was the last time you spoke with Janice Wilson?"

"She and my son, Joe, were once engaged. They separated two months after Joe met Tara."

Tara saw Mike's nostrils flare. Conrad wasn't answering the question. The detective leaned forward in his chair. "Do you know how to find Miss Wilson?"

Tara held her breath, and Logan squeezed her hand tight. Pemberton shook his head, and she sensed he hadn't lied. He couldn't lead them to Janice.

"Can you think of a reason Miss Wilson would kidnap Nicholas?"

Pemberton slapped his hand on his desk. "For ransom."

"But I don't have any money," Tara protested.

"What about the money Joe embezzled from me?" Pemberton declared.

Logan and Mike looked at her with questions in their eyes. Her stomach lurched. "What are you talking about? You know I'm broke. Besides, Joe wouldn't have stolen from his own father."

"I let him handle several investments for me. Shortly before Joe drowned in the water scooter accident, the money disappeared."

She suddenly recalled the conversation when she'd overheard Joe talking about large sums of money. Again she sensed Conrad was speaking the truth. "Why didn't you ever say anything?"

He drilled her with his stare. "I assumed you knew."

No wonder he believed she wasn't a fit mother. He'd probably thought Joe had included her in his thievery. "Why didn't you go to the police?"

Pemberton's eyes flashed with rage. "And disgrace the family name?"

Mike cleared his throat. "Let's get the facts straight. Joe embezzled a substantial amount of money before he died. Then his old girlfriend kidnaps his son."

As she worked through the clues, Tara's voice rose. "Do you think Janice believes I have this money?"

Mike nodded. "Janice must have known Joe stole from his father. When Joe didn't give her the money, she assumed you got it."

But for Janice to know Joe's secrets, her husband must have been seeing her while they were married. Finally, Tara understood her husband's coldness. But if he'd never loved her, why had he married her instead of Janice?

"Was there a ransom note?" Mike asked.

"No." Logan moved toward the phone. "I'll check my machine and see if anyone left a message." A moment later he shook his head.

"When was the last time you saw Janice Wilson?" Mike asked Conrad.

Tara spotted the slightest hesitation in his voice before he spoke. "Haven't seen her in years."

Liar. Her hands trembled, but Logan squeezed tight, and she imagined courage flowing from him to her. She raised her chin and spoke strongly. "You realize your grandson's life could be at stake. If we don't find my son because of your lies, you'll have his death on your conscience."

Conrad held her stare, then looked away. At first she didn't think her words had had an effect on him, but she was wrong. He slumped back in his chair and spoke wearily. "Janice came to my house three weeks ago. She said she knew where you were and she needed money, so I hired her to spy on you."

She raised her chin and stared him straight in the eyes. "To prove I'm not qualified as a parent, so you could take me to court and get custody of Nicholas?"

"Yes. When you started having trouble, I thought you'd faked all those problems so the court would feel sorry for you. I never dreamed Janice..."

The lines on Conrad's face deepened in the harsh light of his study. He looked older and genuinely sad.

"You had no idea she intended to kidnap Nicholas?" Mike asked.

"The child's my grandson. I would never want harm to come to him. Although I knew Joe embezzled my money, I wasn't sure whether he'd shared with his wife. For my grandson's sake, I offered to give her money, even though I suspected she had plenty—but she refused to accept my help. Wouldn't let me see my grandson, and he's all that is left of our family."

Guilt stabbed her conscience. Perhaps if she'd been strong enough to welcome Pemberton's help, he would have come to accept her. By running away, she'd separated him from his grandson. And now, neither of them had Nicholas.

"This is all very interesting, but it isn't helping us to find Janice," Mike interrupted. "Did she ever call or write?"

"I only saw her that one time." Pemberton spoke slowly but with conviction, and she believed him.

"How did you pay her?" Logan asked.

"In cash. I never saw her again."

Tara thought hard. Joe had told her little about Janice, and he never kept memorabilia around—not even a picture of his mother. "What about Joe's old stuff? Did he have high school or college yearbooks, old letters, that sort of thing?"

Pemberton tilted his head toward the stairs leading to the bedrooms. "There's a box of pictures in his closet. I've never looked through it."

Tara and Logan left to search Joe's old room. Dust-free soccer trophies and plaques with faded newspaper clippings dominated the walls. A picture of Joe and his parents rested on the corner of his desk. No doubt the memories of his son stealing from him made the thought of cleaning out the room too painful for Conrad to face, because it appeared as if he hadn't touched a thing since the day his son moved out.

Logan opened the closet, and a baseball glove tumbled into his hands and bats rattled onto the floor. Old clothes dangled over camping gear, skis and scuba equipment.

"What's that?" Tara pointed to a box on the top closet shelf.

Logan took it down, and when they discovered it was full of pictures, they returned to Mike and Conrad in the study. Dumping the contents of the box onto the big desk, Logan stared at the hundreds of pictures and letters with a frustrated grimace.

"What are we looking for?"

"A picture of Janice Wilson could be helpful," Mike answered. "Or a letter with a return address."

"The woman is clever," Pemberton said. "She graduated Princeton Phi Beta Kappa. She's been planning this for a long time, I'd guess," he added slowly. "Not only did she take Nicholas, she tried to frame me."

Tara hoped Pemberton no longer thought her the enemy, because they still needed his help. They had to find Nicholas.

Besides, any family made her feel less alone. "You had the perfect motive to kidnap Nicholas, and Janice knew it," Tara added, throwing several postcards from Europe into her discard pile.

Conrad Pemberton had suffered through all this, too. First, his only son had stolen from him. Then he died. His daughter-in-law had refused to let him see his grandson. And then Conrad had been threatened with jail for a crime he hadn't committed. For the first time, she found herself sympathizing with the old man.

She tried to make an apology. "If we find Nicholas—"

"*When* we find him," Conrad corrected her.

"I think it would be nice if he got to know his grandfather."

Mike's beeper went off. "Mind if I use your phone?" the detective asked.

Helpfully, Pemberton gestured to the phone on his desk. But if she expected Conrad to apologize for sending Janice to spy on her, she'd have to wait for another time.

After Mike grunted into the phone, he hung up. "I've got to go. We just broke the kidnapping ring, and they need me downtown. I'll question the suspects about Nicholas, although I don't think the cases are related."

Ten minutes after Mike left, Conrad tossed a picture of Janice and Joe onto the table with a triumphant snort. "Here she is in her blond stage."

Tara grabbed up the picture with a gasp. Janice Wilson was Marge Henley—her crazy back-door neighbor. The woman had moved into her neighborhood, pretended to be a friend, and all the while she'd planned to take her child.

She glanced again at the picture. As Marge, Janice must have dyed her hair or worn a wig. The resemblance between Janice and Tara was amazing with both of them blond. They could have been twins.

Leaning over her shoulder, Logan peered down at the picture. "The hair and heavy makeup sure made her look different from the woman in that picture."

Something clicked in Tara's mind. "She impersonated me. She's the one who made me lose my job. And remember when she claimed she was pregnant?"

Logan let out a low whistle. "I'll bet she was planning on taking the kid then. And remember at the soda fountain she claimed her husband's name was Joe."

"She didn't take the breakup with my son well," Conrad told them. "For months afterward she called here two or three times a day. Joe took her calls, and they would speak for hours. She loved my son to distraction. I thought he was making the biggest mistake of his life when he married you," Pemberton admitted.

"Why *did* he marry me?" Tara wanted to know the truth.

"I don't know." Conrad let out a sigh. "We weren't close. He thought I interfered too much in his life."

"Can't imagine why," Logan said wryly.

"Raising a child isn't easy," Conrad said. "After Joe's mother died, I had to be both mother and father. I was wrapped up in my businesses, but I did the best I could. It wasn't enough. I could never give Joe enough. So I encouraged him to marry Janice, thinking her love would make him happy. She was from our social class. She went to the right schools. Was the same religion. She clearly adored my son."

"And now this paragon has kidnapped your grandson," Tara said scathingly while she flipped through Joe's yearbook. Although antagonizing Conrad was stupid, her nerves were drawn so taut she couldn't help snapping at him.

He blinked and stared into space, seemingly lost in memories. "Janice was a nice girl then. What father wouldn't encourage his son to marry such a woman?"

No one answered his rhetorical question. Logan started reading through two years of postcards from

England. Tara double-checked the discard pile which was growing higher and higher as the evening wore on.

"When Joe broke their engagement, I thought he did it to spite me," Conrad told them.

Tara was hearing more about Joe now than she'd heard during her marriage. From the way her father-in-law spoke, she guessed he had many regrets.

Didn't everyone? If only she hadn't left Nicholas alone, she'd have him tucked safe in bed. If Janice hurt him...Tara couldn't complete the thought. *Don't torture yourself.* It won't help Nicholas. Won't bring him back. And she sensed the answers were tied to the past.

If the way Joe had treated her was any indication, he'd probably regretted their marriage, too. Had he jilted Janice and married her to spite his father?

Somehow all the pieces of the puzzle didn't fit. Joe had pursued her, and he'd been elated when she'd gotten pregnant. But if he hadn't cared about her, why had he married her? Had he known his disapproval had made her lose faith in her own ability to cope?

In the months after he'd died, she'd regained much of her independence, and she wouldn't give up. Every time she thought of her missing son, though, her confidence dipped and tears began to form. Thank God she hadn't gone through the past few days alone.

No matter how much she wanted to blame her preoccupation with Logan for the disappearance of her son, she couldn't do it. Janice had stalked Nicholas for weeks. Sooner or later, Tara would have had to leave him, and the woman would have struck. *Please don't let her hurt him,* she prayed.

Her gaze went from the picture of Janice in her hand to Logan, her anchor in this terrible storm. She watched as he held a letter up to the light, squinted at the tiny print and frowned. Although his business hinged on completing that shopping center bid by tomorrow, she knew he hadn't considered leaving her since Nicholas disappeared. She'd found a warm, compassionate man who'd stick by her no matter what.

She could no longer keep up the wall that separated Logan from her heart. She went to him, his warm glance making her welcome, and his arm curled around her waist to draw her to his side.

Resting her head against the corded strength of his chest, she tried to take comfort in the regular beat of his heart. Staring down at Pemberton's desk, she wondered if they were on a wild-goose chase. Most of the carton had been emptied, and though they'd found several more pictures of Janice, they'd yet to find an address or phone number.

Pemberton reached across his desk, tumbling the three pictures they'd set aside. Tara bent to pick them up and spotted writing on the back of one of them. Slowly, with excitement raising her voice, she read the words aloud. "Our dream home."

Chapter Thirteen

With shaking hands, Tara flipped the snapshot over and searched past the smiling faces of Janice and Joe to the picture's background.

"What is it?" Logan asked.

She'd never missed the drafty old place that held only bad memories. "That's the house Joe and I lived in after we married," Tara explained. "And the back message, 'Our Dream House,' isn't in Joe's scrawl, but in a woman's writing with elegant loops."

"So?" Conrad shoved his chair back from his desk and poured himself a brandy. "Joe bought the house before you married him. It doesn't take a genius to figure out Janice helped him choose."

"But don't you see?" Too excited to stand still at Logan's side, Tara paced. "The house I lived in with Joe had been Janice's dream house *before* we married. But this picture was taken in the past year, probably right before Joe died."

"But if this picture is recent, why would it be here at his father's house in a box of old things?" Logan asked.

"Joe came here often," Pemberton offered. "He said he didn't want his wife snooping into his business."

Tara held up the snapshot. "This picture is recent. We repainted the exterior before Nicholas was born. Joe didn't want his baby breathing in the fumes."

"My son was having an affair?"

"That's not important anymore," Tara said. What Joe had or had not done no longer hurt her. Only getting her son back mattered. "Look at the message on the back, 'Our Dream House.' Janice intended to move into my house *after* Nicholas was born."

Logan's brow creased. "You think Joe was going to divorce you?"

Pemberton threw his glasses on the table and rubbed the bridge of his nose. "There's never been a divorce in my family."

Tara felt her heart go out to her father-in-law at what he considered his son's treachery. If they didn't have to find her son there would be no sense in raking up the painful past.

"Besides, how is this going to help us find Nicholas?" Conrad asked pointedly.

"After Joe died," Tara said in a measured tone, "I had to put the house on the market. I couldn't afford the mortgage. When I put the house up for sale, it sold in one day."

"One day? Was the buyer Marge Henley?" Logan asked, obviously following her train of thought.

"I don't know. The buyer preferred to remain anonymous, and I just needed the money. Joe's lawyers handled the closing. But it would make sense if

Janice had bought the house. And I think that's where she has my baby."

Conrad stared at the picture. "I'll call Detective Scott and have him get a search warrant."

"Have them search the house in Harden, too," Logan said.

"Won't that take hours?" She noticed Logan shaking his head, silently signaling her to be quiet, but his eyes gave nothing away.

Conrad reached for the phone. "Be patient. Let the police take care of it from here."

Patient? How could she sit around twiddling her thumbs when that crazy woman had her son? While Conrad called the police, she turned to Logan. "Detective Scott might need a search warrant, but we don't."

Obviously the old man had listened to her every word. He hung up the phone, stood and walked to a closet. "I'll get my gun."

Logan swore under his breath. "I don't think bringing a firearm is a good idea. We have to outsmart her."

For once, Tara agreed with Conrad. "We don't have time to play games. She's had Nicholas for hours. He could be cold, hungry, or..." *Don't think it.* Surely Janice Wilson wasn't crazy enough to hurt Nicholas.

"The woman made several passes at me," Logan said. "She must be lonely."

"What are you going to do?" Pemberton asked. "Knock on the front door and offer to take her to bed?"

Tara looked to Logan for answers. "And what reason would you give for showing up on her doorstep in the middle of the night? Especially in a location she doesn't expect?''

Logan lifted his brows and shot her a conspiratorial smile. ''You're underestimating my powers of persuasion. I learned a little acting in Hollywood.'' Continuing with a laugh, he added, ''Good thing I did, too, since I many need to resume my old line of work—''

Tara's hand went to her mouth. She turned to Conrad and said, ''If Logan doesn't bid on this shopping center, he won't get a job he needs to carry him through the summer.''

''Son, you get my grandson back for me, for us,'' Pemberton said, ''and I'll see you have enough contracts to keep you busy for the rest of your career.''

''Thanks.'' Logan tugged Tara to the door. ''Come on. We're wasting time. We'll work out the details of how to get into the house on the way.''

Although she had no idea why Logan seemed so sure of himself, she agreed he could be very persuasive. Before they left Conrad, he'd convinced her father-in-law to stay put, promising to call him the minute they had Nicholas safe. Surprising herself, she gave her father-in-law a kiss on his leathery cheek.

SHE DROVE AWAY with Conrad's whispered words, ''You'll get your baby back,'' repeating over and over in her mind.

Unable to sit still, she fidgeted on the seat, giving directions while Logan drove at breakneck speed. She turned the heater to high, but the heat couldn't warm the chill that had settled over her like a veil. Luckily, there wasn't much traffic at this late hour. Although he'd said they would make plans on the way, she didn't want to speak and distract him from driving.

Apparently comfortable driving and talking, Logan broke the silence. "Tell me about the layout of your old house."

She hadn't expected to ever return to this neighborhood. The creepy old houses brought back ugly memories, and she spoke to distract herself from the sudden shiver that seeing them produced. "It's a two-story Victorian—just like Conrad's, only smaller. The bedrooms are all upstairs. Downstairs, there's a den, dining room, kitchen and back porch."

"Neighbors?"

"They mind their own business. No one's within shouting distance since the yards are more than three acres."

When he swerved around a bread truck, she let out a gasp, then spoke quickly so he wouldn't sense her fright and slow down. The sooner they reached Nicholas, the sooner he'd be safe.

"Janice must be crazy." Tara closed her eyes for a second when the road curved and Logan steered a straight line to cut off the corners. "Why does she want Nicholas now? Why did she hide Nicholas in my closet? Why did she want me to lose my job? Why did she shoot at us?"

He didn't answer her questions. Instead, he exited the freeway, pulled off onto a two-lane road and asked one of his own. "If Janice lives there, where do you think she'd put Nicholas?"

"Upstairs. The nursery is next to the master bedroom."

He risked a glance at her. "I want you to wait in the truck."

"But—"

"Hear me out. If I can convince Janice I'm interested in a romantic evening, I might get her to take me upstairs to see Nicholas."

"I know the house better than you do," she shot back.

"Look, I don't want you hurt."

She refused to let him talk her out of it. Nicholas's life could be at stake. "You distract Janice and keep her downstairs. I'll climb the oak in the back and sneak into the bedroom."

Logan's voice was laced with concern. "And then what? It would be better if she never saw you. Janice could have a gun. Can you climb down the tree with Nicholas?"

He'd asked a valid question. She couldn't safely climb down the tree with her baby. But leaving Nicholas with Janice wasn't safe, either.

Once again, she thought how much she appreciated his help. Sneaking into the house would be terrifying. A squeaky door or a loose floorboard could alert Janice, but Logan's distraction would make Tara's task easier.

She recalled the huge old tree, the thick branches so evenly spaced, and wished she had the baby carrier to strap Nicholas to her chest. "I'll climb down with one hand if I have to. It's the next street." She pointed.

Logan shut off the lights and cruised past the house. The upstairs looked dark, but downstairs several lights were on. Before he returned to the house, he stopped the truck and pulled Tara across the seat. He riveted his gaze on her face, and her pulse jolted at the thought he was once again willing to risk his life for her son.

They had parked under a street lamp, and the yellow glow reflected a smoldering flame in his eyes. Desperate, she clung to him, taking comfort in sharing this ordeal with him. His warm mouth captured hers, demanding a response. Flinging her arms around his neck, she drew him closer, drawing on his strength.

She tried to learn his taste, his scent, the hardness of him, by heart. Gradually over the past few days, her attraction to Logan had deepened to love. She'd been powerless to resist his virile appeal, and even now, when she was desperate to find her son, she found spare thoughts for Logan's safety.

"Ready?" he asked.

"Don't forget to call her Marge, not Janice."

"I've got my lines straight. After all the passes that woman has made, I should be able to convince her I'm interested. Give me two minutes before you start to climb that tree." He turned the lights back on, boldly drove down the street, and turned into the drive as if he'd every right to park there.

After he shut off the truck, Tara ducked across the front seat but cracked the window open to hear what was going on. Logan knocked on the door, and she held her breath for what seemed like a long time.

Anticipation surged through her. Had they guessed right? Did Janice own Tara's old house?

Finally Janice answered, and Tara remembered to breathe.

"I decided to accept your offer," Logan said in that low, sexy voice Tara found so irresistible.

"How did you find me?" Janice asked, a tinge of suspicion coloring her tone.

"Now, that is a long story, and it's a cold night. Are you going to invite me in? Offer me a drink as a reward for my ingenuity?" he teased.

"My husband isn't home," Janice admitted cheerfully.

The door opened wider, Logan stepped inside, then it shut firmly, leaving Tara alone in the night. She no longer heard voices, but remained still to give them time to amble past the front windows. As she waited for the seconds to tick by and her pounding heart to calm, the truck's cab started to cool.

Slowly, she opened the truck door and slipped out. Not wanting to make a sound, she didn't shut the door. Merging with the shadows of the house, she slipped around the side to the backyard. A neighbor's dog barked, and she froze, rooted to the spot. What if Janice had a dog?

When no outside lights flashed on, she peeked around a hedge, tilted her head and gazed up at the huge oak. Damn! Janice had built a second-story balcony along the back bedrooms with the trunk of the tree extending through the middle of the deck.

Was there room to ease between deck and tree trunk? Were the branches sturdy enough to hold her farther out on the limbs? From the ground, in the dark, she couldn't tell. She circled the tree trunk once to survey the branches.

Choosing the best way up, she reached for the first limb. Her hand slipped. Climbing the icy and snow-covered tree would be harder than she'd thought.

After removing her gloves, she tried again. The frozen bark bit into her fingers, but her grip felt more secure. Pulling herself up a notch, she scraped snow off the tree in search of a secure foothold. Although the climb down should be easier, she'd have Nicholas in her arms.

Pausing to catch her breath once she'd climbed up five more feet, she realized that she would somehow have to find a way to tie her baby to her or they'd never make it back down.

One step at a time. Despite her numb fingers, a trickle of sweat rolled down her spine. She glanced down. If she fell, she'd never survive landing on the concrete patio furniture below. *Climb. Don't look down.* After several minutes' more exertion, she was two stories up and she'd bumped the underside of the balcony.

Moonlight couldn't reach her, and she was forced to feel around for an opening between the tree and the surrounding decking. While the builders had left the tree growing room, there was not enough space for her to squeeze by.

She'd have to inch her way out on the sturdiest branch she could find and pull herself onto the deck. Afraid to let go for even a second, she edged her hands on a branch and slid her feet along the bough under her.

The two branches didn't run parallel, and she put more weight on her hands. Her foot slipped. Her fingers tightened on the overhead limb while her dangling feet fought to recover her balance.

Refusing to give up, she tried again, making her way under the lip of the deck. A thin branch cracked and broke beneath her hand. Frantic, she grabbed another. *You're almost there.*

After another five inches of progress, with one hand, she clutched the rim of the deck. Kicking her feet on the bottom cross timber for leverage, she scampered up and over the balustrade.

Her chest ached from breathing in the cold air. And she was forced to rest on her back for a moment, gazing at the stars. She checked her watch, fearing she'd taken far too long to make it this far, but she couldn't read the time in the dark.

Hurrying to her feet, she sidled to the house. Janice had installed a French door that probably replaced the upstairs linen closet. Tara reached for the doorknob. Locked.

Next she tried a window, and that, too, was locked. A sob rose in her throat. What should she do? If she broke the glass, would Janice hear her and grab Nicholas before she did?

There had to be another way. Hovering near the French door, she examined it more closely. Her fingers felt for a loose pane of glass. Perhaps she could remove the caulking around a pane.

She'd left her purse in the car, and she didn't have a hair clip handy, and her pockets were empty. Damn!

Think. All she had was an empty wooden deck, snow and an old tree with a few of last year's acorns the squirrels hadn't eaten yet. She trod quietly to the tree, broke off a branch, returned to the door and set to work.

After a few minutes of scratching away the caulking, the pane fell silently into her hand. Ignoring the numbness in her fingertips, she stretched her arm through the opening and unlocked the door.

The new door didn't creak, and she stole inside, her heart pounding. Barely daring to breathe in the dusty hall and give away her presence with a sneeze, she crept down the familiar corridor toward the nursery on tiptoe, thankful she didn't need a light.

Logan's voice drifted up from downstairs. "Are you sure your husband won't be returning home tonight?"

At least she didn't have to worry about running into anyone else. If Logan could keep Janice talking, she should be safe.

Feeling her way down the textured wallpaper in the long hall, she made herself walk slowly. Janice could have redecorated, and she didn't want to risk bumping into anything in her haste to find her son.

Was he here? Her nerves felt frayed and frazzled. Although she didn't think Janice would put a baby in the guest room, Tara opened the door and checked to be sure. A streetlight shone through the windows, revealing no changes in the ugly green-and-gold room. The same furnishings that Joe had picked out still remained. When she didn't find what she sought, she moved on down the hall.

A creak behind her rooted her in place. Had it been the oak brushing against the balcony? Or her overactive imagination?

She'd skipped the bathroom and another linen closet when she thought she heard a sound that didn't belong. Like the whisper of air hinting at danger before a blow struck, she sensed something, someone, behind her.

Downstairs, she heard Janice's soft laughter. "I wanted you from the first time we met."

Tara had sensed that desire for Logan in the other woman and recalled wondering why a married woman, supposedly pregnant, would so openly go after Logan. She imagined Janice's red nails wrapping around Logan's neck, drawing him closer like a black widow about to consume her mate.

"I felt an irresistible chemistry between us," he replied. "I fought the attraction, but your allure was just too strong. I couldn't get you out of my mind."

Don't lay it on too thick, Logan, or the woman will never believe you.

Janice laughed. "Did I invade your dreams? Keep you up at night?"

Logan's voice oozed sugar-coated charm. "Must you know all my secrets?"

Two more rooms to check. First the master bedroom, then the nursery. The noise she'd heard must have been snow shifting on the roof. Maybe a baby turning over in his crib.

"I love a man with daring," Janice cooed. "Did you learn any bedroom stunts?"

Tara imagined the woman licking her lips and about to pounce. Logan could more than take care of himself, but she needed to hurry before Janice tried to drag him upstairs to bed. Even Logan could only delay for so long before following through or backing out of what he'd promised.

Later, after she found Nicholas and returned to the truck, she'd set off his truck alarm to signal him. But so far she hadn't seen one sign of her baby. Could they have been wrong?

A blast of cold air hit her, as if someone had opened a window upstairs. The tiny hairs on the back of her neck prickled. Holding her breath, she held absolutely still and listened.

Nothing except the two voices from downstairs, their tones reduced to intimate murmurs now. She could no longer afford to delay. She had to stop jumping at every creak and groan.

Stepping over the threshold into the master bedroom in the dark, she moved toward the bed to make certain the large room didn't hide a crib in a darkened corner. Miniblinds across the windows filtered an eerie light across the room. Plush carpet, deep as swamp mud, kept her footsteps silent.

From out of the night, a hand shot out and clamped over her mouth.

No! No one would stop her from rescuing her son. Futilely she tried to bite the hand over her mouth. She'd come too far to let anyone stop her now. She dug her elbow into her attacker's stomach. His breath went out of him with an oof. He reached for her again and she fled across the bedroom—not fast enough.

He grabbed her jacket and yanked her back hard. Wildly, she groped the dresser for a paperweight, an alarm clock, anything to use as a weapon.

Her hands came up empty so she used her feet. Wrapping his ankle in hers, she tripped him, and they fell in a tangle of arms and legs. Terror made her scramble to her feet. He grabbed her jacket. She shrugged it off and bolted across the room. She didn't try to scream, needing every breath of air to escape.

Sensing her assailant close behind her, she flicked on the light to blind him. Without looking back, she lunged away, her heart beating out of control. He grabbed a lock of her hair, bowing her down and around to face him.

Without straightening, her knee came up to catch him in the groin, but her attack glanced off his thigh, and he shook her so hard her teeth knocked together. Still, she tried to raise her frozen hands up to claw his face, and her foot stomped his instep.

He yanked her by the hair until tears filled her eyes. Her head jerked up to gaze straight into her attacker's face, and her eyes widened in recognition. It wasn't possible. The blood drained from her face. He sneered down at her with an all-too-familiar go-to-the-devil twist of his lips.

Her husband had come back from the dead.

Chapter Fourteen

Tara's thoughts swirled and refused to focus. Joe couldn't be real. And yet she felt his fingers painfully yanking her hair, smelled his expensive cologne and saw the amusement in his cruel eyes.

Although the handsome image of her husband had tarnished, there could be no doubting his identity. With his short brown hair starting to thin at the temples of his wide forehead and dark circles under his eyes undisguised by new glasses, her husband appeared to have aged ten years in the last twelve months.

But his lip curled in the same old arrogant sneer. "Did you miss me? No words of love for your dead husband?"

Fear for her life vanished in a maelstrom of confusion. For a moment, she ceased to struggle. How could he have done this to her? How could he have done this to his son? "You faked your death?" she sputtered.

"Go to the head of the class." He snickered. "I planned it all so carefully. Leaving pieces of the water scooter for the beach patrol to find. Picking the right hour to disappear, so the riptide would carry my body out to sea.''

''But why? Why did you do it?''

''Father's money, of course. He was so stingy. After I refused to come into the family business, he never gave me a penny. But the old fool trusted me to invest his funds into a stock portfolio. Instead, I outsmarted him and helped myself to the money, taking my inheritance early.''

He'd put all of them through months of turmoil for greed. Although she'd never mourned Joe, her father-in-law had thought he'd lost his only son. Now more than ever, Tara felt sorry for Conrad.

Logan and Janice must have heard the noises, and they now entered the master bedroom to investigate. Even then Joe didn't release the painful grip on her hair.

''Let her go,'' Logan demanded.

''Ah, the new boyfriend. Didn't know she still had a husband, did you?'' Joe clenched her tighter against his chest.

What would those words do to Logan? Allison had told him she wasn't married, and when he'd found out his old girlfriend lied, the betrayal had crushed him.

Despite the pain, she twisted to glance at Logan. ''I didn't know.''

''Of course you didn't know,'' he agreed easily. ''Now, let her go,'' he demanded again.

Joe's hand tightened painfully in her hair, jerking her head and forcing her gaze back to his scornful amusement.

Help came from an unexpected quarter.

With her nails extended, Janice, her eyes livid with fury, charged Joe. "You can't have her! I've waited too long for her to ever come between us again."

Forced to release Tara or have his eyes scratched out, Joe shoved Tara to the floor. She rolled across the dusty brown carpet, and Logan helped her up.

All the while, Janice screamed at Joe, "You always loved her more! Miss Goody-Two-Shoes, the baby-maker."

The raving woman made no sense, but Tara wasn't about to stay for more explanations—not when Nicholas might be in the next room. Tugging on Logan's hand, she scooted out the door to leave Joe with his crazy girlfriend.

Flicking on the light in the nursery, she moved straight for the crib in a room that had not changed one iota since she'd decorated it more than a year ago. Except for the dust, it was eerily the same—not just the wallpaper and carpet and light fixtures. Somehow Janice had replaced the baby furniture Tara had taken to her new house with the exact same furniture in the same colors.

So what? The woman was insane. None of it mattered if her son slept safely under the blanket in that crib. Let him be there. The five steps across the room seemed to take forever.

Logan beat her to the crib, his face lighting with pleasure. "Nicholas!"

Safe. Her son lay on his back, sucking his thumb and clutching his blanket. She'd never been so glad to see anyone in her life. Snatching him to her chest, she nuzzled her cheek against his baby skin.

At the sound of footsteps, she pivoted. Joe and Janice had followed them into the nursery. Janice pointed a gun directly at Nicholas. "Give me the baby, or I'll shoot."

From the distance of four feet, the woman couldn't possibly miss. Tara felt dizzy. To lose Nicholas again after finding him was more than she could take. Walking slowly toward Janice, she cradled her precious child.

"Why do you want my baby?"

Janice laughed wickedly. "He was never yours. He was always meant to be mine."

"What is she talking about?" Tara jerked her head around to Joe, who stood in the doorway.

"Janice couldn't have children," he explained, giving her the answer to questions that had plagued her for months. "When I walked into that video store and realized how alike the two of you looked, I decided you should have our baby."

"You married me because I looked like her?" She couldn't believe what she was hearing. Nausea pummeled her like a tidal wave. No wonder he'd acted so cold. No wonder he'd changed the very day they'd married. He'd never loved her. His whole reason for marrying her was to get her pregnant and steal her child.

"Marrying someone out of my social class was a bit embarrassing, I admit, but since you gave me my son, I'll forgive you."

He would forgive *her!* Anger surged through her, washing away the nausea. He wouldn't get away with this. How dare he think he could take her son?

Out of the corner of her eye, she saw Logan edging toward Janice. *Keep them talking.* Maybe he could get the gun away from her.

"You married me, planning to fake your death and kidnap my baby?"

"I planned to simply divorce you."

"But you didn't want to share Nicholas and risk joint custody," she guessed.

"True. And after I found a way to get my inheritance early, I decided to tie up all the loose ends at once. I have a new identity waiting for me in a new place, and I've come back for my son. No one will suspect a dead man of kidnapping."

Her stomach felt like he'd struck her with a baseball bat. "You would have taken Nicholas away from me, and I'd never have seen him again."

"Oh, stop the maudlin act," Janice ordered. "I deserve to have Nicholas. I worked hard to get him, even learned how to pick locks. You can have ten more brats if you want them. Nicholas is mine."

Janice pointed the gun at her face, her smile more terrifying than Joe's had ever been.

Logan edged another step closer. *Keep talking,* she told herself.

"One child cannot replace another." If she lost Nicholas— No. He was hers. She'd carried him inside her for nine months, given birth to him. He was her blood, her flesh, and they couldn't have him.

Joe came up beside Janice and leaned against the baby wallpaper with sailing ships he'd picked out so long ago. "I tried to make the eventual separation easier on you. That's why I didn't want you to hold or feed him," he admitted, as if commenting on a newspaper editorial and not the kidnapping of her son.

"How kind," she muttered, unable to keep the sarcasm from her tone.

Damn! Before Logan could sneak closer and disarm her, Janice motioned him back with her gun. "And now you can say your goodbyes for good. Give me the child or I'll shoot him."

Nicholas's eyes widened. "Bad."

Joe frowned, and Tara had seen that look too many times not to know Janice's threat annoyed him. Yet he didn't tell the woman to put down her gun.

A thousand dull knives stabbed her chest at what they were forcing her to do. Logan nodded, encouraging her to hand over Nicholas, but she could see pain and anger and frustration in his eyes. She didn't have a choice. As much as she yearned to keep her child, watch him grow to adulthood, his safety would always come first.

"Mama?" Nicholas squirmed against her.

"Soon he'll be calling me Mama," Janice taunted.

Tara handed the woman her son, tears slipping down her cheeks. Angrily she wiped the tears away with the back of her hand. She had to do something. But what? The woman had her son and a loaded gun. From the look in her triumphant eyes, she appeared ready to use it.

"Mama." Nicholas wriggled and Janice held him tight, too tight, and her son yelped.

The woman had wanted Tara's house, Tara's husband, Tara's child. And once she'd met Logan, she'd wanted him, too. If only she could use the woman's insane jealousy against her before she hurt Nicholas. And help was coming, if only Mike got here soon.

She forced admiration into her tone. "You were clever, leaving Conrad's glove and then his cuff link behind as evidence. But I never understood why you hid Nicholas in the closet."

Janice laughed, but the gun never wavered in her hand. "After Logan foiled my first attempt, I saw the worry on your face. And I thought it only right that you should suffer like I had."

"How did you suffer?" Logan asked sympathetically, his tone filling Tara in on the fact he was up to something.

"My friends thought Joe broke our engagement over that piece of white trash." She gestured to Tara with the gun. "I suffered one humiliation after another. First she married him, then she had his child while I sat and waited alone. She had him in her bed, and I was alone."

Logan took a step toward Janice, his face sincere. Whatever he had in mind, she would do her best to play along.

"Joe was wrong to make you wait," Logan said. "You're more than enough woman for me. We wouldn't need children to make us complete."

"He's lying!" Joe's cheeks turned red with outrage. "Don't let him confuse you. You have everything you want. Me. Nicholas." He raised a briefcase in his hand. "Father's money. We can have it all."

"He doesn't love you like I could," Logan crooned. "Give him the kid and the wife he wanted so badly. I'd never make you wait for me. I'd never leave you alone. We'll fly to Rio and be married by morning."

Janice considered Logan's offer, licking her bottom lip. "You don't want a baby?"

"I only want you," Logan insisted.

Tara held her breath and dared to hope his deception might work. Logan was a damn fine actor. He'd missed his calling in stunt work.

"This is ridiculous!" Joe smacked the briefcase against his leg. "He's trying to trick you." He put his arm on her shoulder in a possessive overture. Janice shrugged him off and backed toward the balcony, juggling Nicholas in one arm, pointing the gun at Joe with the other hand.

"Remember all those nights you had to spend alone," Tara interjected, trying to keep Janice off balance. "Joe couldn't keep his hands off me."

"That's a lie. I never touched her once she got pregnant."

Tara forced a catty smile to her lips. "You don't believe that, do you?"

Logan took a step toward Janice, his hand outstretched. "Give them the baby. All we need is each other."

"Are you crazy?" Joe shouted. "He's trying to turn you against me."

Confusion clouded Janice's eyes. She retreated until her back thudded against the French doors.

Nicholas cried out in protest at Janice taking him from his mother. Furious, Janice shook him. "Stop it. I can't think with you screaming."

"Let them have the baby. He's more trouble than he's worth," Logan suggested softly.

"No!" A wily look gleamed in her eyes. "If I can't have a baby, neither can she." Janice plopped Nicholas over her shoulder, her forearm supporting his bottom. Transferring the gun to the hand holding Nicholas, she opened the French doors and backed onto the balcony until she leaned on the railing.

Nicholas kept twisting around, looking for Tara. She ached to comfort him.

Janice dangled Nicholas over the edge.

Oh, God! She meant to drop him onto the concrete below. Her son would never survive. Tara tensed, intending to lunge for her baby—knowing she'd never make it—when Joe walked straight toward Janice.

Joe held out his hand to Janice. "The strain has been too much for you. You're not yourself. There's no reason to kill my son."

"I want everything Tara has. I want her house, her lover, her son."

"And what about us?" Joe asked her softly.

"You were spying on me in our home!" Janice's eyes glittered. "Were you trying to take Nicholas away from me?"

Joe took a step toward Janice and the baby. "Of course not."

"Stay back." She waved the gun wildly. "Or I'll destroy all of you, and myself, too."

"Give me my son." Joe grabbed for Nicholas.

Then everything seemed to happen in a blur. Janice raised the gun at Joe and fired. He grunted and slumped against her, knocking her off balance. The three of them teetered on the edge.

Nicholas screamed. "Mama! Mama!"

Panic clawed her insides. And she lunged forward. Too late. She was too far away to save her child. For a moment she thought they might regain their balance, prayed they'd drop her son on the deck.

Then the three of them toppled backward over the railing.

Out of nowhere, Logan seemed to fly through the air right over the railing.

Alone on the balcony, she rushed forward on wobbling knees, her heart roaring like a locomotive in her ears. At the thud of bodies hitting concrete below, she thought she'd be sick. Running to the edge, she looked onto the patio, but it was too dark to distinguish individuals amid the snow.

Reeling in shock, she raced down the hall, tripping her way down the stairs. As she threw open the back door, her heart thundered. She didn't want to look, but had to know if Nicholas or Logan had survived.

Two adult bodies lay sprawled across concrete benches—Janice and Joe. Janice's neck lay crooked at an odd angle, her sightless eyes staring at the night sky, her mouth twisted. Joe lay unmoving beside her.

Where was Nicholas? And Logan?

Could they have fallen free of the patio and landed in the snow, their bodies buried? They could have survived the fall and be suffocating.

"Up here," Logan called from somewhere overhead.

She looked up to see him hanging by a branch from his knees. Upside down in the tree, about fifteen feet above the patio, he cradled Nicholas in his arms.

"You'll have to catch him." Logan sounded confident that she could do it.

A branch cracked and Logan and Nicholas swung. There was no telling how long he could hold on to her son from his position, and the branch could give way any second.

Fear made her hesitate. If Logan dropped Nicholas to her and she couldn't catch his weight, her baby would never survive.

"You aren't strong enough," Joe groaned. "You're too weak."

His taunts sent a surge of adrenaline racing through her. After swiping snow off the concrete table with her palm, she climbed onto the table and raised her arms another three feet closer to her son. In total, she guessed Nicholas would drop about seven feet.

"Try and break his fall," Logan gasped. "Ease him down. Catch him at the end."

She understood what Logan wanted her to do and struggled not to tense. *You can do this.* She shook the tension out of her hands and again lifted her arms toward Nicholas. "Ready."

Nicholas's feet kicked. "Uh-oh."

"Now," Logan warned her.

Nicholas dropped feet-first like a sack of potatoes. She clutched him at the waist while he was still over her head. Remembering Logan's instructions, at first she merely tried to break Nicholas's fall. When her baby fell to about eye level, she pulled him toward her chest. He was so heavy. He slammed into her, knocked wind from her lungs, but she didn't let go. Her feet slid out from under her, and she landed on the table, her bottom smacking hard concrete.

"Go boom?" Nicholas giggled.

She couldn't speak past the lump in her throat, but tilted her head back to watch Logan swing safely down from the tree hand over hand like a champion gymnast. No matter how many times she'd thought it through, she'd never really comprehended how he'd managed to dive off the balcony, catch Nicholas and hang on. Once again he'd risked his life and saved her son.

He came to her, limping worse than usual and looking better than a man who'd almost died should. He didn't spare a glance at Janice. "Are you all right?"

"We're both fine. Is your leg okay?"

Before he reached her, he stooped and his fingers searched for a pulse in Joe's neck. "He's gone."

Although he'd tried to save Nicholas, she had no feelings for her dead husband. He'd caused everyone so much grief. Now it was time to put the past behind them. Time to build a future for her son with the man she loved. Although neither of them had spoken words of commitment, their bonds of love had grown so strong, none were needed.

She shivered and he helped her from the table. They walked into the house, Logan's arm around her shoulder. He put in a call to 911 in the kitchen while she checked Nicholas more thoroughly. Her son was fine. She couldn't find a bruise on him.

A car pulled into the driveway. Mike had finally arrived to deal with the bodies.

Logan put down the phone and limped closer. His deep voice reverberated against her ear, sending a crackle of warmth through her. "I just want to know one thing."

"What's that?" She slid into his arms with Nicholas in the middle.

"Am I through auditioning for a part in your life?" he teased.

"Hmm. Let's see." She pretended to consider. "Do you want the part of daddy, husband or lover?"

Nicholas put in his two cents. "Dadada."

Logan chuckled, his laughter more potent than wine. "Greedy man that I am, I think I could handle all three."

She raised her lips to his. "You're hired."

HARLEQUIN®

I N T R I G U E®

43 Light St.

Outside, it looks like a charming old building near the Baltimore waterfront... but inside lurks danger and romance.

The winner of the 1994 Career Achievement award for Romantic Mystery, Rebecca York, returns with...

PRINCE OF TIME

A devastating avalanche was the last thing Cassandra Devereaux expected while hiking up a mountain in the Alaskan wilderness. Only by ducking into a cave was she able to survive. But when the cave is sealed by the ensuing ice and snow, Cassandra isn't at all prepared for the sight that awaits her deeper in the underground lair....

Don't miss #338 PRINCE OF TIME, in September, wherever Harlequin books are sold. It's Rebecca York's most unusual book ever!

LS95-2

OFFICIAL RULES

FLYAWAY VACATION SWEEPSTAKES 3449

NO PURCHASE OR OBLIGATION NECESSARY

Three Harlequin Reader Service 1995 shipments will contain respectively, coupons for entry into three different prize drawings, one for a trip for two to San Francisco, another for a trip for two to Las Vegas and the third for a trip for two to Orlando, Florida. To enter any drawing using an Entry Coupon, simply complete and mail according to directions.

There is no obligation to continue using the Reader Service to enter and be eligible for any prize drawing. You may also enter any drawing by hand printing the words "Flyaway Vacation," your name and address on a 3"x5" card and the destination of the prize you wish that entry to be considered for (i.e., San Francisco trip, Las Vegas trip or Orlando trip). Send your 3"x5" entries via first-class mail (limit: one entry per envelope) to: Flyaway Vacation Sweepstakes 3449, c/o Prize Destination you wish that entry to be considered for, P.O. Box 1315, Buffalo, NY 14269-1315, USA or P.O. Box 610, Fort Erie, Ontario L2A 5X3, Canada.

To be eligible for the San Francisco trip, entries must be received by 5/30/95; for the Las Vegas trip, 7/30/95; and for the Orlando trip, 9/30/95.

Winners will be determined in random drawings conducted under the supervision of D.L. Blair, Inc., an independent judging organization whose decisions are final, from among all eligible entries received for that drawing. San Francisco trip prize includes round-trip airfare for two, 4-day/3-night weekend accommodations at a first-class hotel, and $500 in cash (trip must be taken between 7/30/95—7/30/96, approximate prize value—$3,500); Las Vegas trip includes round-trip airfare for two, 4-day/3-night weekend accommodations at a first-class hotel, and $500 in cash (trip must be taken between 9/30/95—9/30/96, approximate prize value—$3,500); Orlando trip includes round-trip airfare for two, 4-day/3-night weekend accommodations at a first-class hotel, and $500 in cash (trip must be taken between 11/30/95—11/30/96, approximate prize value—$3,500). All travelers must sign and return a Release of Liability prior to travel. Hotel accommodations and flights are subject to accommodation and schedule availability. Sweepstakes open to residents of the U.S. (except Puerto Rico) and Canada, 18 years of age or older. Employees and immediate family members of Harlequin Enterprises, Ltd., D.L. Blair, Inc., their affiliates, subsidiaries and all other agencies, entities and persons connected with the use, marketing or conduct of this sweepstakes are not eligible. Odds of winning a prize are dependent upon the number of eligible entries received for that drawing. Prize drawing and winner notification for each drawing will occur no later than 15 days after deadline for entry eligibility for that drawing. Limit: one prize to an individual, family or organization. All applicable laws and regulations apply. Sweepstakes offer void wherever prohibited by law. Any litigation within the province of Quebec respecting the conduct and awarding of the prizes in this sweepstakes must be submitted to the Regies des loteries et Courses du Quebec. In order to win a prize, residents of Canada will be required to correctly answer a time-limited arithmetical skill-testing question. Value of prizes are in U.S. currency.

Winners will be obligated to sign and return an Affidavit of Eligibility within 30 days of notification. In the event of noncompliance within this time period, prize may not be awarded. If any prize or prize notification is returned as undeliverable, that prize will not be awarded. By acceptance of a prize, winner consents to use of his/her name, photograph or other likeness for purposes of advertising, trade and promotion on behalf of Harlequin Enterprises, Ltd., without further compensation, unless prohibited by law.

For the names of prizewinners (available after 12/31/95), send a self-addressed, stamped envelope to: Flyaway Vacation Sweepstakes 3449 Winners, P.O. Box 4200, Blair, NE 68009.

RVC KAL